UNDER THE SUN

Erik Jay

UNDER
THE
SUN

U.S. DISTRIBUTOR
DUFOUR EDITIONS
CHESTER SPRINGS,
PA 19425-0449
(215) 458-5005

Peter Owen · London

ISBN 0 7206 0654 3

PETER OWEN PUBLISHERS
75 Kenway Road London SW5 0RE

First published in Great Britain 1986
© Erik Jay 1986

Photoset and printed in Great Britain by
Redwood Burn Limited, Trowbridge, Wiltshire

ONE

1

It was mid-afternoon. In Africa. The sun bounced hard off the whitish façade of the National Federal Hotel as he mounted the front steps.

'Top of the African afternoon to you, old boy,' said someone in the doorway.

John Peters looked up through the heat to see Colonel Brendan Murphy, red-faced as ever.

'How's life?'

'Never felt better.' Then he said, 'There's been an incident.'

A raucous air-conditioner spluttered and blabbered above them, its dribble soaking into the pock-marked, mildewed concrete. It was difficult to hear and to concentrate.

'What happened?' asked John Peters.

'Some Red Cross people were killed or wounded in the advance on Mbonawi.'

'Hell!' he muttered. He had his own plans for the next few days and this would certainly disrupt them.

'WAWA,' said Brendan, before continuing. 'A signal came in on the Red Cross network. The details are utterly confused. The Government forces deny responsibility, saying a Red Cross doctor was killed in cross-fire and that it was his own fault for being outside the hospital building. Other relief workers who witnessed the scene and survived claim that he wore correct Red Cross insignia and was shot in cold blood by a Government officer who gave every impression of being punch-drunk. In short, the reports are as usual unclear and contradictory. Perhaps your friend at the Ministry knows more.'

'I'll call him, if the telephone works, if I can reach him, if he does know, and if he's prepared to tell me. If so, I'll ring you back right away.'

'I shall be in my room,' Brendan answered as they passed through the lobby.

'Hallo.' From out of a mist of pungent scent, like an animal on heat, a girl presented a toothpaste grin and projected her body at them, its impressive protuberances bulging above from a tight lace blouse and below from the parcelling of her wrap.

'Don't jump up and down, beautiful, or you'll give yourself a black eye,' said Brendan.

'Beautiful, me,' replied the girl.

'My friend thinks so,' Brendan said, nodding at John Peters.

John Peters smiled at the girl and walked with Brendan Murphy towards the elevator.

'Comforts for the troops,' Brendan said as they entered. 'Want a drink?'

'I'd better try the Ministry. But thank you.'

The two men felt warmly towards each other. They drank together, joked together and came close to friendship. But something inhibited Brendan from sharing confidence; he used flippancy to shelter a more serious and vulnerable self. He mocked his position as secretary at a golf club, to which he had retired from the army. Keeping the boys replenished at the bar and chatting up the girls was his job description. Only mention of his daughter brought out the tenderness in his disposition. He had married late and the explanation he gave was typical. 'You married?' he had asked John Peters early in their acquaintance, and when the answer was negative, had gone on to say, 'Got to marry before you're forty, you know, or they'll think you're queer or incapable.' 'When did you marry?' John Peters had inquired. 'When I was thirty-nine, the eleventh hour, the witching hour,' Brendan had replied with a laugh. In response to the question 'Any children?' he said gently, 'A daughter', with such obvious joy and affection, but had stopped short as if this daughter belonged exclusively to a distinct emotional world.

When John Peters entered his room the steward was already busy turning down the sheets, although it was only 4.15.

'Good evening, sir,' the steward greeted him.

'Hallo, steward, how are you?'

'Good.'

He waited for the steward to go.

'Telephone done ring, sir,' said the steward.

'Who was it?'

'Don't know, sir.'

'An outside call or from inside the hotel?'

'Don't know, sir.' He paused. 'Maybe outside call.'

'Why do you say that?'

'Don't know, sir.'

'Never mind.'

'Never mind, yes sir,' and he left the room.

The telephone rang, then went dead as John Peters lifted the receiver. Behind the phone a cockroach scuttled for safety, but a slipper caught him on the floor. The pus oozed from its brittle casing as from a broken chocolate cream.

John Peters dropped the slipper with its slime and picked up the receiver once more. He asked for an outside line and endeavoured to reach the permanent secretary at the Ministry of Defence. He passed through several operators, who were busy chatting to friends, who misunderstood him, gave him incomprehensible replies, wrong extensions, and finally, at last, the right number. The permanent secretary was still in his thirties, like John Peters, though this was only one reason why they understood and liked each other.

'Is not on seat, please,' replied a secretary.

'Will he be back this afternoon?'

'Don't know.'

'Thank you.' And he replaced the receiver. It was no use trying the private number; the only person ever at home was his wife-for-the-capital. She was invariably there but never knew where he was or when he would return. Instead he called room service for ice. While he waited, the phone rang again. Unlikely as it was, it might be the Ministry, having failed to reach him earlier.

'John Peters speaking.'

'This is General Bergström,' came a singsong voice.

'Good afternoon, General.'

'I am the new Swedish general, representative to the Joint Inspector Group.'

'Yes, I know. Welcome to Africa.'

'I am calling you because I am calling an emergency meeting this evening about a very serious incident which has been reported. The meeting will be at 1745.'

'Thank you, General. I shall be there.'

'Thank you,' said General Bergström, and rang off.

Behind the telephone the dead cockroach had been metamorphosed into a reddish puff-ball, a small fur of living ants.

John Peters washed and changed. Then he gathered his courage to phone Bola. They had known each other for three months or more. When they met at a social function she was recently divorced from an American and had returned to Africa after two years abroad in New York. For the daughter of a ruling family, marriage to a former Peace Corps volunteer, a young middle-class American at the start of his career, had proven too restrictive. They had lived modestly, without servants of course, entertaining hardly at all, and Bola's dress allowance had been ludicrously inadequate by her inherited standards. She was offered a post in public relations with her national airline; he refused to let her accept on the grounds (she said) that the African pilots would take advantage of her. She was to remain at home, dressed for his return in the evening, with ice cracked into the bucket and the television on.

She found life increasingly oppressive, and they had agreed to separate.

John Peters was immediately attracted to Bola. She had the splendid physical properties of an African woman in full bloom and was cosmopolitan also. While she knew that her parents, prominent socially and politically, had no wish to see her again involved with a white man, after years out of Africa she balked at the manner in which most African men, even among the educated, treated their wives and their women. John appealed to her.

Bola was keen to seek out old friends and re-establish herself at home; this was best done without the company of an outsider. John Peters had his work and expected to stay but briefly in the country. It suited them both that he travelled frequently. Although they sometimes pretended otherwise, neither Bola nor John Peters sought close emotional involvement. They saw each other when he was in the capital after inspection tours and she was free and so disposed. But she came to resent his being often unavailable. She was accustomed to having her way; in Africa, at least, her family were seldom thwarted in their desires. Reluctantly she accepted absences on tour, but refused to tolerate other commitments when these conflicted with her plans. The affair would have been short-lived, had it not been sustained by a powerful physical attraction.

'Hallo,' came her warm African voice.

'It's John.'

'I tried to call you earlier. You weren't in.'

'I went for a walk.'

'For a walk! Where?'

'Just to get out of the hotel.'

'Are you coming round? We could have a drink.'

'No. We've got an inspectors' meeting in a quarter of an hour and then there's that dinner.'

'What dinner?'

'I told you. The Norwegian ambassador.'

'Oh, yes. But why are you having a meeting now? It's Wednesday, isn't it? I thought your meetings were on Mondays and Thursdays.'

'This is an exceptional meeting.'

'So I won't see you tonight. Do come in good time tomorrow for the party.'

'I may not be able to come.'

'But that's ridiculous. We arranged it specially.'

'I know. It's not my fault. I shall probably have to go to the front tomorrow.'

'Why?'

'There's been an incident at Mbonawi. Some Red Cross people were shot, allegedly by Government troops.'

'Why this fuss about Red Cross people, with all the others being killed? It's their own fault, anyway. They shouldn't be there. What business is it of theirs? They're foreigners. They're spies, that's what they are.' She sounded angry. Then she said, 'What has it to do with you?'

'The Government denies responsibility, so there'll have to be an investigation, I feel certain.'

'Just because they're white. They should investigate why Africans are being killed. But why do you have to go? Can't the others do it? We arranged the party specially, you know that. When will you be back?'

'In two or three days.'

'You'll be back by Saturday. We are going swimming.'

'I hope so.'

'It can't take that long.'

'You know the transport difficulties we sometimes have.'

'I don't think you have to go, really.'

'Couldn't we see each other tonight?' he suggested.

'You just said you had a meeting now and a dinner later. How can we?'

'I could come round after dinner.'

'It'll be much too late.'

'I'll leave on the stroke of eleven, or earlier if there's a chance.'

'No, that's too late. That's silly.'

'Then I won't see you before my return from Mbonawi.'

'It's your fault.' And she hung up.

Behind the telephone he noticed that the puff-ball had vanished and the shell of the cockroach with it.

There was a knock on the door. The steward with the ice at last. 'Ice blocks, sir,' he announced.

It was too late for a drink. John Peters made to put the ice in the refrigerator for later. The bucket refused to fit.

'If you take away the cover, it will enter,' said the steward, moving close his strong-smelling person.

2

Shortly before 5.45 the inspectors forgathered in a small
conference-room on the first floor of the hotel. The one
window was haphazardly covered by a length of green baize
to prevent outsiders peering in during confidential dis-
cussions, or to spy on classified documents and maps. The
oblong table that furnished the room was modestly decorated
with a further expanse of green baize, nibbled by termites and
humidity blotched. There were no other ornaments, no documents, and the only map in the room was standard issue car-
tography of the Federation divided into regions and states as if
had been before the civil war. It bore no reference to the fighting zone. A loud-mouthed air-conditioner made conversation
difficult without greatly reducing the temperature in the room
when it was full.

The Government, accused in the international press of
genocide and indiscriminate killing of civilians in its campaign
to prevent secession in the north, had invited certain friendly
and neutral countries to send 'inspectors'. In the words of the
chief minister, who resented what he termed the libel, 'The
intention is that you see things for yourselves and then tell the
world what it is really like.' The Government had assumed
that a series of brief tours to the main theatres of military activity would produce the desired testimonial, after which the
inspectors could leave. But the Northern propaganda machine
had craftily implied that this would be the signal for earnest

extermination, the moment of genocide. So the inspectors remained, a thorn in the flesh of the Government, which had come to consider their presence an indignity, an irritation to the field commanders, ineffectual fellow-travellers in the anti-Government relief community, and a minor embarrassment to themselves. Recycled senior officers came and departed. To impress the Government, world opinion and each other, most received reclassification, like upgraded second-hand cars. Few stayed long. Most had outgrown the age when the rigours of life at the front exercised any appeal.

The United Kingdom's Major-General Martin (he was really a brigadier) had been there longest. He knew Africa and Africans intimately after a long career in colonial armies. Colonel Brendan Murphy, an Irish, retired lieutenant-colonel, recalled from his job at the golf club, had also had years on the continent, including service with international peace-keeping units. He was delighted to be back where he could feel useful and important. The Polish colonel knew war and soldiery from generations of experience. The Swede, who had just arrived, had been temporarily promoted to major-general; he was an expert in underground fortifications. The Government had also asked the World Organization to provide an observer.

The inspectors said 'Good afternoon' and 'Good evening' to each other. Some shook hands; the Polish officer half saluted. Only the Swedish general wore uniform.

'Gentlemen,' said General Martin in a parade-ground voice. The inspectors ceased talking, scraped their chairs around the table, arranged themselves in comparative comfort and waited.

General Martin began: 'I had hoped that our liaison officer, Major Adeboli, would be here. I imagine he has been held up in the traffic. But I think we should proceed with our meeting. It is now', he looked at his watch, '5.50.... 'I have already explained to General Bergström,' he continued, glancing at the general, 'that it is the practice of the Joint Inspection

Group to rotate its chairman every week, and it so happens that it is the turn of the Swedish inspector. Since General Bergström arrived only the day before yesterday, I offered to seek an alternative arrangement, but he, in the fine tradition of his own service, felt it would be wrong to evade responsibility. It gives me great pleasure to welcome General Bergström to the Group and to our group. I am sure he will appreciate, as I have done, the remarkable team spirit which pervades our work as members of JIG. This I see as reflecting the proud military traditions from which we are all drawn in our own countries,' he nodded at each in turn, 'Sweden, Poland, Ireland and, of course, Britain. Indeed, it is to be expected among brother officers. Naturally, I should not wish to exclude our good friend from the World Organization.' He looked towards John Peters and, as if to imply that this was an immoral complication, he added, 'He contributes the political dimension which is inevitable in our present task, although as a military man I sometimes prefer to be without it.'

John Peters caught Brendan's eye across the table. They had both heard this many times before. It was General Martin's habitual quip, his standard introduction to Peters: to name his unit and rank. No army man exists without his rank. John Peters looked round. Soldiers playing soldiers. Strange how the military self-image cuts across frontiers and how military notions of loyalty, duty and discipline constrain other feelings. These men related to each other like officers of sister regiments, yet knew little of each other. He had asked General Martin once whether the Polish representative was married. 'No idea' had been the reply. It was not so much lack of interest as a sense of what was proper. They were cast in a mould of conformity, and private life lay beyond the professional soldier's pale.

General Martin was marching on: 'Without further ado I should like to give the chair to General Bergström.' He rose from his chair at the head of the table.

General Bergström moved round from his place at the side,

shook hands solemnly and sat down. 'It is a great honour', he proclaimed with a marked Swedish lilt, 'to be president of the Joint Inspector Group. It is not only in this country and at home but in the world that the people are looking for us to know the truth. My name is General Bror Bergström. I am coming from Sweden. In Swedish my forename is meaning "brother" and I hope you will call me "Brother".'

The Polish officer shrugged one shoulder and whispered to Peters, 'I'll call him "brother" if he calls me "comrade".'

General Bergström elaborated on the mandate of the Joint Inspection Group as if recapitulating a brief he had been given upon appointment. The others listened politely. In any case they were waiting for the Government liaison officer to arrive.

The Polish officer said to Peters, 'If in four months I do not know this . . .', and he shrugged both shoulders.

'I am only coming before yesterday in Africa,' General Bergström continued after a pause, 'and I am not yet knowing the country very well. A very serious incident has been reported today and I am calling this meeting for that. Some places are still difficult for me to pronounce and I prefer therefore my friend General Martin explain to you all about it. General Martin, please take again the chair.'

'Do you want a receipt for it?' said General Martin.

'What?' asked General Bergström.

Martin sat down and began: 'I recall during the war the C-in-C Mediterranean issuing this signal: "Everyone wishes everybody else a Merry Xmas and a Happy New Year – and now let's have no more of that."'

There was a mild titter.

General Martin went on: 'I had hoped that Major Adeboli would have arrived by now, but I imagine he will be here any minute. Meanwhile we are required, as General Bergström has said, to give our attention to a serious incident. It is reported that during the recent advance of Government troops on the town of Mbonawi in 2 Div Sector there was fierce fight-

ing and, unfortunately, a Red Cross worker, a doctor, Dr
Campbell, I believe, was killed in the cross-fire. He was apparently outside the hospital building itself, it is not clear for
what reason. One or perhaps two other relief workers inside
the hospital were slightly wounded in the sporadic shooting
which continued after the main assault – presumably by rico-
cheting bullets.' General Martin was proud of being well
informed. He expected, as a general, to have the best
intelligence available and to know more than his staff.

'The hospital is situated just below a strategic hill, which
was where the fiercest resistance was encountered during the
assault. According to the surviving Red Cross personnel,
they all remained as instructed on hospital premises during
the attack and wore their Red Cross insignia clearly displayed.
There was also a Red Cross flag to mark the compound. When
the main fighting appeared to be over, the doctor-in-charge
tried to identify himself to the advancing Government troops
and was allegedly shot down in cold blood by a junior officer
who was shouting and screaming. This is according to Red
Cross reports. I can only conclude that, in accordance with
our terms of reference, an investigation of the facts is both
imperative and urgent. Gentlemen, I invite any com-
ments. . . .'

While General Martin was still speaking the door opened
surreptitiously. The inspectors snapped their heads round as
if in response to a military command. An African officer in
an over-starched uniform entered, clicked his heels and
saluted flamboyantly. 'Good evening, sirs,' he said and smiled
broadly.

'Good evening, Major Adeboli,' General Martin responded. 'You were held up in the traffic, I imagine.'

'Yes, sir. Sorry. But I always say, sir, "Better late than
never".'

The general was not amused. 'Jide,' he said, 'we have been
discussing the incident at Mbonawi in which it is reported that
a Red Cross relief worker – a doctor – was killed, and one or

possibly two others were wounded. Have you the latest information?'

'No, sir.'

'The inspectors are convinced that the incident warrants prompt investigation by the Group. As you know, the account received from Red Cross sources is at variance with that offered by the Government forces. This means a JIG team going to Mbonawi as soon as possible – I warned you earlier. Given the hour, we have decided to leave tomorrow morning by the first flight. Were you able to send a signal to the div commander?'

'Yes, sir.'

'Do you know if he received it?'

'No, sir.'

'Will arrangements have been made to receive the inspectors in 2 Div?'

'I hope so, sir.'

'When will you know?'

'I don't know, sir.'

'This may mean our setting off before confirmation is received.'

'Yes, sir.'

'And what about travel arrangements?' General Martin asked.

'I have requested bookings on the flight to Umuadan tomorrow morning. Departure is at 0700 hours,' replied Major Adeboli.

'Is this confirmed?'

'Not yet, sir – but, I always say, sir, "No news is good news".' He beamed.

'We must assume it will be. The flight to Umuadan is a commercial flight, but how is it proposed that we should travel on from Umuadan to Mbonawi?'

'We are sending a signal to the rear commander requesting an aircraft from Umuadan to Beningo, and from there transport will be by jeep.'

'How long will it take altogether? The flight to Umuadan is little more than an hour, I believe.'

'Yes, sir. Not more than one day.'

'Good. We should like to be in Mbonawi tomorrow evening to meet the divisional commander and to hear from him what happened. You say you have already sent a signal?'

'Yes, sir.'

'We shall, of course, also wish to speak to the wounded Red Cross personnel and others at the hospital during the advance.'

'Yes, sir.'

'I think that is it, Jide. Any other questions, gentlemen?'

A split second of silence and General Martin announced, 'In that case the team will leave from the main entrance to the hotel tomorrow morning at 0615.'

'Journalists,' someone said.

'Oh, I nearly forgot,' General Martin blurted out. 'Do we take journalists? I say "yes". I believe to exclude the press inevitably distorts the impression of open inspection we seek to convey. If there is no objection I propose we take a couple of pressmen from the main news agencies, depending on the space available. They can draw lots.'

There was a mild murmur but no one objected.

'Agreed,' announced General Martin and closed the meeting.

'Hallo, Jide, you old rogue,' said John Peters as he passed him.

'Hallo, John.' Jide slapped his palm heftily in an exuberant African handshake and tickled it with his forefinger. 'Still organizing the world?'

Major Jide Adeboli played soldiers too. But his African exuberance, his impulse to laugh often and loudly gave to his drummer a livelier beat.

3

Shortly before eight o'clock, the hour for which he had been invited to dinner, John Peters went to find his car. There was no sign of either car or Enduke, the driver. He decided to try for a taxi. At that moment the car roared up to the base of the hotel steps, came to an abrupt stop and a grinning Enduke opened the door.

'Where on earth have you been?' asked Peters.

'I am somewhere which is very far.'

'And why are you so late?'

'Jam 'em for street, sir.'

John Peters looked nonplussed.

'Too much car,' Enduke explained.

'Traffic jam!'

'Yessir.'

'Did you take the message to the cable office?'

'I don' do it.'

'You did? Or you didn't?'

'I don' do it.'

Enduke was in fine driving form. He showed dangerous flair. John Peters was reminded that General Martin's predecessor, at the end of his tour, had given Enduke a generous tip. 'Here,' he had said, 'take some driving lessons.'

'What, sir?'

'Did you ever take those driving lessons?'

'I don' do it.' And he turned round with a grin while an

20

oncoming car swerved to avoid them. Both drivers swore loudly.

They arrived at the Norwegian ambassador's residence before a quarter past eight. Peters was admitted by an impressive Nubian servant made all the blacker by his impeccable white gloves and a white uniform detailed with high-gloss livery buttons.

'Good evening, sir,' the servant said. 'Please sign book.'

There were three men already in the drawing-room when Peters entered. One he did not know; the others were the ambassador and the newly arrived Swedish inspector, now dressed in civilian clothes, of which the only remarkable feature were over-stated regimental cuff-links riding like bosses beyond the sleeves of his jacket.

'Good evening, Mr Peters,' said the ambassador. 'How good of you to come.'

It had surprised John Peters to find so consummate a diplomat in an unappealing post peripheral to his country's interests. The Norwegian ambassador was urbane. He was also intelligent and perceptive, the kind of diplomat who derives pure satisfaction from a dispatch elegantly phrased, succinct without forfeiting relevant detail, and heightened by insights into the impact of influences beyond the public view. The ambassador's genuine interest in the work and his low golf handicap combined to give him an influential position in the community. He was able to establish important contacts. All of which might have been largely academic had not civil war broken out. Of a sudden his own country with its humanitarian tradition became deeply involved in relief to refugees and persons displaced by the war, to the suffering women and children. The ambassador's personal acquaintance with leaders of the secessionist north as well as in the National Government offered him a unique advantage, which he was able to use effectively because of his utter professionalism, by which he remained well informed, analytical and personally detached.

'I think you already know General Bergström,' the ambassador was saying.

'Yes. Good evening.'

'May I present Reverend Jørgensen, secretary-general of Scandinavian Relief Operations, better known as Scandro.' And turning to the other, the ambassador, added: 'Pastor Jørgensen, Mr Peters is from the World Organization and is at present assigned to the Joint Inspection Group, like General Bergström.'

'Have you been long in the country?' Pastor Jørgensen asked.

'Nearly six months, which makes me quite an old hand,' he replied. 'And you?'

'I come and go. I have been coming and going for many years.'

The ambassador interrupted to explain that since his wife was away in Norway he had not invited any ladies, and he thought that a stag evening would provide a better opportunity for serious talk about the situation.

While drinks were unobtrusively served General Bergström engaged Pastor Jørgensen in conversation about the recent drought in Scandinavia. According to the pastor it had been the driest summer in living memory and the consequences for agriculture could only be guessed at, although certainly grave. In his part of Sweden the general maintained that, while it had been unusually hot and rainless, disaster was not imminent. Just before he left for Africa he had experienced two downpours that were exceptionally heavy for the time of year. The pastor had heard of rain farther north; it had yet to reach the southern parts of Scandinavia.

A sliding door opened almost imperceptibly while they were talking and the white-liveried servant with white gloves glowed blackly in the opening. He nodded to the ambassador.

'Gentlemen, shall we go to table?' said the ambassador.

The dining-room was candle-lit, the air-conditioning system struggling audibly to maintain the temperature at a level low enough to offset the impact of food and wine.

'You will forgive me if it is only a simple dinner,' the ambassador commented as *coquilles Saint-Jacques* were set before them. Afterwards there was veal. 'Food is quite a problem here. We have to import almost everything.'

John Peters drank with increasing pleasure several glasses of a crisp white wine and then a claret which he could not positively identify but was evidently château bottled.

General Bergström, sipping his wine with ladylike daintiness and refusing a second glass, began: 'We are leaving in the morning for Mbon...'

'Mbonawi,' completed Pastor Jørgensen.

'I hear there has been an unfortunate incident there,' said the ambassador.

'That is what we will investigate with the Joint Inspection Group,' General Bergström offered.

'Does anyone know what really happened?' asked the ambassador.

'According to the Government,' said Peters, 'the Red Cross doctor who was killed was outside the hospital at the time of the advance and was shot in the cross-fire between Government troops and the Northerners who held a strategic hillock just behind the buildings. The line between the opposing forces may have been unclear, as often happens, and there must have been wild shooting. One can see how these things could happen.'

'In reality, my dear sir, it was rather different,' interrupted Pastor Jørgensen. 'I have received a full report from the surviving relief workers at Mbonawi. Apart from the wounded man there were three other medical and relief volunteers in the hospital to witness the events, including Mrs Campbell, the wife of Dr Campbell who was killed. She is herself a nurse and a remarkable, dedicated person. So was he. One of the finest. A man of exceptional courage and discipline and with a capacity for work which was altogether extraordinary. He was ready to die of overwork.'

For a moment John Peters imagined them. Dr Campbell, rigid but devoted and fully convinced of the values, the self-sacrificing values, which he sought to impose on others. She, never far behind him, a no-nonsense person replete with good works, a have-you-been-a-good-boy-this-morning hospital matron equally sure that what they were doing was right. A difficult pair for Africa to digest, and yet you had to admire people who had the conviction to act out their beliefs in difficult and dangerous conditions, who were prepared to give all for what they believed in.

Jørgensen continued: 'What occurred was this. The assault was over and the firing had ceased, but for some sporadic shooting which always accompanies any engagement with National Government troops. They appear to be under no orders to conserve ammunition and are generally ill-disciplined. At this point, Dr Campbell, who wore his Red Cross badge prominently displayed, thought that as leader he should emerge from the hospital buildings and make known to the local commander of Government forces that a Red Cross team was on the premises and ready to provide medical treatment for civilians in need and to distribute relief supplies to displaced persons. You will remember that Red Cross and other relief personnel have been specifically requested to stay put during battles, to remain in compounds marked with Red Cross insignia, and not to move along roads or through the bush with those who flee the fighting. This is to underline their impartial humanitarian role, and it equips them to give help more effectively and quickly.

'As Dr Campbell came into the open, a small group of Government soldiers, shouting and shooting, entered the hospital compound. He showed his Red Cross emblem and called to them in English that he wished to address an officer. None apparently understood the language, although the Red Cross emblem must have been obvious to them. One of the soldiers then pointed his rifle at Campbell and the others began to jeer. Campbell could only assume that he was being taken for a white mercenary, and he knew what that meant.

'Again he showed his Red Cross emblem, repeated "Red Cross" and "doctor" loudly and distinctly, and then said "officer" once more. The group moved menacingly towards him, and when they were within feet of where he stood his ground, a flushed, excited, drunken officer stepped ahead of the other soldiers and addressed Dr Campbell in a local language. Of course Campbell did not understand a word and continued to repeat "Red Cross" and "doctor" since those are terms commonly understood even by those who speak no English.

'The others in the hospital watched as tension mounted. Campbell, having failed to communicate through words, finally held out his hand as a gesture of friendliness, and at that moment the officer, if he was one, shot him dead. The volley of bullets from his automatic weapon not only killed Dr Campbell but sprayed the hospital. The other soldiers also started shooting and it was during this episode that a Red Cross worker inside the hospital was wounded.

'Pandemonium ensued and no one seems clear how the major commanding the sector suddenly arrived on the scene and was able to restore order. He ordered the unruly troops out of the hospital compound and then communicated in good English with the surviving members of the Red Cross team.'

When Pastor Jørgensen had completed his exposé, the air-conditioning seemed suddenly noisier and there was a clatter of cutlery as the guests finished eating and plates were removed from the table.

Then General Bergström said, 'That is why we must go to Mbonawi,' he pronounced the name in three distinct, precise syllables, 'to see what is really happening and to tell the world.'

Pastor Jørgensen looked knowingly at the others and stated, 'They will never let you find out the truth. You will see, you will see. The National Government will never admit that an officer shot a Red Cross doctor in cold blood and sprayed a hospital with bullets. When you come there it will be too late to establish real events. And they will have a story for you. Believe me.'

'We shall be there tomorrow evening already,' said General Bergström.

'I doubt it. I doubt it very much,' said Jørgensen prophetically.

John Peters explained that there were often delays when travelling and that communications were difficult.

Bergström, as if to change the subject, began again: 'Now that they have captured Mbonawi, it will not be long before the end. It is the capital and headquarters of the Northerners.'

'That doesn't follow,' the ambassador said. 'The war has been a slow one. When it began, everyone expected it to be over in six weeks. That was eighteen months ago. They advance very slowly.' He paused, appeared to reflect, then went on: 'Estimates in this part of Africa are invariably suspect. Take the census figures, take the number of refugees, take the calculations of those who fled north.' He paused again. 'Let me give you an example. Before hostilities broke out I had a conversation with Colonel Kidumi – the leader of the Northerners,' he added for the benefit of General Bergström.

'Ah, yes, I know,' said General Bergström.

'I have known Colonel Kidumi for a long time,' the ambassador continued. 'He's an intelligent man, very intelligent, educated in England – at Cambridge or Oxford, I think. He was always proud to say he had been there with our crown prince. I asked him how many Northerners really returned to the north as refugees after the riots. Two million, he told me. Are you sure? I asked him, because I have often considered those figures exaggerated. I know this country. Then Kidumi said that 300,000 actually registered, and that in the circumstances it had to be assumed that there were twice as many refugees as those who registered – so 600,000, and, in Africa, only the family heads reported. Since every family head spoke for at least three persons, we arrive at a round figure close to two million. I raised an eyebrow when he explained this, but he seemed to take his arithmetic seriously.'

'I believe him,' said Pastor Jørgensen. 'You should see the camps.'

'As to the fall of Mbonawi,' John Peters suggested after a short silence during which the wine went round, 'it is not yet clear what that will mean. The Government forces or the Northerners may take a town and vaguely control the roads linking one place in their hands with another, but much of the country remains no-man's-land. And because it is so simple to ambush a patrol when only the narrow tarmac is yours, advances are ambiguous and slow. Mbonawi has been taken and retaken by one side or another twice already since the war began. On one occasion after it had been in Government hands for some days, the Government continued airdropping supplies to the garrison for a further week after the Northerners had recaptured it, because no one on the staff knew for sure who was in control.'

Pastor Jørgensen interrupted. 'The Northerners have the support of the local population. When their forces move, they can count on the people. The village folk do not trust the Government. They have been deceived too often by promises never implemented, by assurances not guaranteed. This is why they fled behind the Northerners' lines.'

'But have they?' asked John Peters. 'My impression is that the great majority remain where they are while the opposing armies move backwards and forwards.'

'The facts show otherwise,' insisted Pastor Jørgensen. 'The vast refugee camps in the north bear testimony to the huge number of innocent civilians who have had to abandon their homes and homelands, whom fear has driven away, whom experience has taught that no Government assurance or Government promise offers any meaningful guarantee that they will be enabled to live in peace and carry out unhampered their daily work in the fields and plantations.'

'The chief minister is adamant', John Peters said, 'that the peace-loving civilian is not an enemy and has to be protected. I believe he means it.'

'It is conceivable that the chief minister means it and he may even wish it,' conceded Jørgensen, 'but do the field commanders and their men? I doubt it. You should see the burgeoning relief camps and hear the stories the refugees tell. I wish you could accompany me on my next visit, indeed I do. Above all you should see the children. Genocide may not be the official policy, but from what I have experienced and heard say, I am convinced that several thousand, four or five, can expect to be killed when the war ends.'

He paused for effect. 'According to our statistics there are now 100,000 persons in refugee camps in the north. Ninety per cent are women and children, the remainder sick old men. We are struggling desperately to keep them alive. The minimum ration per adult should be 595 grammes a day. But the Government blockade obstructs our efforts and makes the relief operation extremely hazardous. I may say we have some very courageous pilots and crews, men who like Dr Campbell are willing to risk their lives, indeed to give their lives for a great humanitarian cause. Our target should be around sixty tonnes, 59.6 metric tonnes a day, even assuming meteorological conditions were to permit night flights seven nights a week, but we consider ourselves fortunate to achieve thirty tonnes. That constitutes the entire combined payload of the aircraft at our disposal and which have the required STOL capacity. It's almost all food, although we need also to ship the equipment and supplies essential to distribute it. That means we are able to meet less than half – less than half', he repeated, 'of the minimum ration. The adults ensure that the children have priority, and you can imagine how little remains. Between two hundred and two hundred and fifty are dying of inadequate nutrition every week. And those are the most optimistic figures.'

There was a moment's silence. It was obvious that General

Bergström had been deeply impressed, and he nodded meaningfully.

'The chief minister', John Peters added, 'has proposed alternative relief routes, both overland and by river – more suitable, incidentally, for bulk supplies. The problem with night flights, for the National Government, lies in the arms and ammunition which can be flown in alongside under cover of relief deliveries and partly also in the equipment and supplies mentioned by Pastor Jørgensen. They include fuel, I think, and spare parts which the Government believes susceptible of diversion to the war effort.'

'Can you really expect the Northerners to accept relief supplies under National Government supervision,' asked Jørgensen rhetorically with a parsonic intonation, 'with the constant fear of blockade and starvation as a weapon of war, the possibility of poisoning, and the opportunities for espionage this would afford?'

'But at least it illustrates the humanitarian commitment of the chief minister and his Government.'

'I think we know better,' Jørgensen stated. 'Two hundred or more persons dying weekly in the camps alone – and the war could go on for years.'

This angered John Peters. Patronizing charity that, however well meant, contributed to perpetuating a war which was killing hundreds of Africans, not just the occasional European, and costing hundreds of thousands their livelihood. He spoke: 'Have you thought that relief flights under shelter of darkness, with cover for the arms and ammunition entering at the same time, as well as the fuel, make it possible for the Northerners to continue fighting, perhaps indefinitely? According to your own figures, two hundred, maybe more, innocent victims die every week. From what you said earlier, four or five thousand might expect to be killed if the war stopped, which would almost certainly occur if there were no more flights, hence neither food nor ammunition. Using only your calculation, simple arithmetic shows that in another year of war twice as many innocent non-combatants, women and children, will die than if the war ended abruptly now. Have you asked yourself whether you might serve the innocent better by ceasing relief flights?'

Jørgensen stalled a moment, then said, 'That is a question I cannot ask myself as a Christian. When I see need, I must meet it.'

There was an awkward pause.

'Will you have some brandy?' asked the ambassador.

Pastor Jørgensen shook his head. Only then did John Peters observe that both the pastor's white and red wine glasses remained full. He had not refused the wine, he had even raised his glass occasionally, but without drinking. Why was it non-drinkers gave off a holier-than-thou aura that was like a drunkard's bad breath?

Later the guests emerged from the air-conditioned embassy into the hot, spongy night. General Bergström asked Pastor Jørgensen whether he was staying at the National Federal Hotel. No, he was at the New. John Peters offered him a lift.

The New Hotel was but a short distance from the residence. There was time only for Pastor Jørgensen to announce that he would be departing during the next day or two (he was not explicit) to visit the north, where the refugee problem would certainly be much exacerbated by the fall of Mbonawi. It was remarkable, he added, how high morale remained among those impressive people, who realized that defeat could mean only extermination of their way of life and their proud independence.

4

John Peters came out into the open air. He realized then that he had drunk more than was sensible. The conversation, the evening, had disturbed him. They had been talking of Dr Campbell who, whatever the circumstances, had just been killed, of relief workers tackling appalling suffering under disheartening conditions, human misery, dying children. Yet it had been so academic, a question of policy, sterilization by statistics. The easiest way of resolving an individual case is to convert it into a statistic; that is precisely what the socialist societies do. Human suffering is sublimated into air freight, payloads and reports. Emotion has to be personal, you feel for individuals, our feelings are too feeble to encompass more. And as the feeling becomes personal, it ceases to be objective, he realized.

He wanted to be close to a person, to touch a warm body, to smell its sweat.

Bola lived near the New. He glanced at his watch. In the half-light he thought at first that he had misread the time: it was after midnight, late to leave a diplomatic dinner and too late to bother Bola.

He hesitated, depressed. The juices rose and ebbed through his body, pumping between his legs. Futile, he knew, to try sleeping.

'To the Rajah, Enduke,' he said to the driver.

'You want go now Rajah Club? I no done chop 'em.'

31

'But I told you to eat.'

'This place too far.'

'That's not true, Enduke.' He must have been with a woman. 'Well, you can eat while I'm at the Rajah.'

The car drove off. They passed the building where Bola lived.

'Enduke . . .' he began.

'Sir?'

'. . . nothing.'

'That house of madame,' Enduke volunteered as they turned the corner.

'I know.'

Signs of the emergency were sparse. Only the black-out, the total absence of street lighting, remarkable in a country of colour and flamboyance, informed the inhabitants of war. And this particular precaution was absurd, its being common knowledge that the Northerners possessed no aircraft with the autonomy to fly within two hundred miles of the capital. A second reminder was posted near every intersection: a man or men in uniform. The unemployed had been issued clothing, pocket-money and weapons, thus making them a force to be reckoned with in civilian life.

Near the Rajah Night Club a group of beggar boys offered to watch his car.

'Me call Samson,' said one. 'Very strong.'

'All 'em call Samson.' Enduke turned to John Peters.

'Me watch 'im good. Give me dash,' shouted another.

The car-watch syndicate implied unmistakably that, were their protective services rejected, they would like pimps scar exposed surfaces, slash the tyres or, according to Enduke, remove the wheels entirely, since tyre-completed wheels had a ready and lucrative market. A car stranded on improvised brick-jacks bore testimony.

He gave the boys something to go away.

On the wall behind, a large poster declaimed *Don't sit on the fence, join the Civil Defence.*

A cripple with leg-stumps rooted in a frame on roller-skates manoeuvred adroitly to corner John Peters as he approached. Another traditional beggar badgered him by the entrance, as he edged uncomfortably through a group of scruffy Africans engaged in uncertain but certainly dubious activity. Two policemen among them looked at Peters with vague hostility.

A dwarf dressed in an embroidered jacket and wearing a vast red turban on his disproportionate head stood guard by the inner doorway. He diverted prospective clients to an improvised pay-desk near the heavy curtain screening access to the sanctuary. Behind him the face of a huge black man hovered menacingly in the half-dark.

John Peters paid and entered a room vibrant with noise, occasional flashing lights and milling people. Koola Ojo and his Starblacks, glistening with perspiration, ejaculated manic high-life music from a low stand. Peters had been to the Rajah only once, in the time before he met Bola, and he had gone to eat their excellent curry at an early hour when dancing had yet to begin. When on some occasion afterwards he suggested to Bola that they go there together, she had been repelled at the mere mention of the place.

Flashing lights apart, it was pitch dark. Only strips, like neon bars, glowed where roller blinds failed to cover the windows in one wall. A hung-over smokiness gave the room its seedy atmosphere with the smell of sweat and stale beer. But the music and dancing were exuberant and vital. A flatulence of life erupted from bodies everywhere. Even the whoriest of the women in over-taut miniskirt and tight blouse had a vigour about her and a sense of movement that were vital and intensely female. Both the men and women moved naturally and gracefully as they danced. At the same time the scene was rank with sex. It smelled of sexuality. Sex pulsed from the rhythm of the music, it wafted from the over-hot musicians who strutted like cocks, reeked from the arms and legs and breasts and bellies on the dance-floor, and oozed from the eyes of girls still waiting.

John Peters was surprised to see sitting alone a young woman with a very pretty face. She smiled warmly when he looked at her. When he asked her to dance, she laughed uproariously and rose. She was many months' pregnant. They danced anyway. She grinned at him frequently, but it was impossible to converse above the high-life uproar. When at last Koola Ojo and his Starblacks had exhausted themselves and retreated, a Ghanaian group emerged to play soul music.

'You like girl?' she asked when they sat with a large Sun beer before them.

'I like you,' he replied.

'Me big belly,' she laughed, pouting her stomach. Hardly changing her expression, she added, 'My man in army. He done die.'

John Peters wondered whether he had understood her correctly. There was so much noise. He said, 'I'm sorry.'

'He soldier man. Good job,' the girl went on.

'Recently?' asked Peters, since she seemed to want to talk about it.

'Las' week,' she replied, 'before 'bonawi.''

She pronounced the name with an unfamiliar accent and it was not clear to Peters whether this was the place he knew.

'What are you going to do?' he inquired.

'Me? Find one more,' she said. Then, looking round, she caught the attention of a girl at the next table and, drawing her over, said, 'This my cousin, Nofi. She no marry.'

Nofi sat down.

'Want more beer?' asked a waiter at once.

'Yes, please,' said John Peters, 'another Sun.'

It came.

'What your name?' inquired Nofi.

'Bill,' he answered, without knowing why he lied.

'I like you, Bill,' said Nofi.

'I like you,' he said politely.

'Nofi done buy some new panties,' said her cousin. 'You show 'im.'

Nofi giggled.

'You show 'im,' said the cousin again and pulled up Nofi's skirt.

Nofi was revealed wearing a pair of orange nylon knickers with a black hand printed on the crotch, the middle finger insinuating itself into a depicted fly. She pushed back her skirt as soon as he had seen.

'You like 'em?' asked the cousin.

'Oh, yes,' he answered, 'I do.'

He went to the lavatory. It stank of urine and the floor was awash. A notice on one wall that read *Do not urinate here* had evidently been interpreted to mean that you should urinate anywhere else. It was a relief to him to escape the nauseating stench in his nostrils and return to the bar.

An African stood by Nofi's table. When he addressed her she shook her head and looked down. He spoke again, harshly, but she remained unmoving with her eyes fixed in front. He left.

When John Peters approached, Nofi smiled up at him and nodded towards an empty chair. 'Sit down,' she said.

'Didn't you like him?' he inquired.

'I like you.'

'Was he too black?' He tried to make it sound humorous.

'You're not.' She brushed his cheek with a finger.

'Nor are you,' he said, noticing the inside of her hand.

'I'm black,' she said and laughed. 'All black. You like me black?'

'I like you,' he replied and touched her forearm gently.

Afterwards he danced with Nofi, whose cousin, she said, had 'gone home for baby'. During a slower number they rubbed each other and she dropped her hand to his trousers, then pushed herself against him for a moment and whispered in his ear, 'You big.'

He laughed.

When they left the dance-floor she turned to him and asked, 'You want go to hotel?'

In the back seat of the car he put an arm round her and she snuggled up to him. 'I like you,' he repeated, 'you're warm.' He took her hand which lay limp beside her and placed it on his thigh. She did not move. 'You don't like me, I think,' he suggested.

Jerkily she shot a hand up his leg, cupped his crotch and kneaded him. Then abruptly she lowered her hand again and left it loosely against his thigh.

John Peters had one arm round her. With his free hand he tiptoed his fingertips from her knee up the inside of her leg, easing aside the short skirt. When his fingers reached the orange knickers, he said, 'Do you need that other hand now?'

'What you say?' she asked.

He edged a finger under the elastic and touched the crinkle of pubic hair, then the membrane smoothness, hot and damp, which released a musky aroma. 'They're pink inside, shocking pink.' The remark came to him suddenly without his remembering who made it.

In the hotel room she removed her wig. Without its elaborate halo her head seemed curiously small and very round. Her real hair, coiled in tight African braids, wiggled like spiders' legs out of a nest. Unhaired and naked but for orange nylon on her hand-covered crotch, she turned professional. 'You give me money,' she demanded. He gave her a wad of dollars, all that remained in his wallet.

At once she lay back and led him directly into action. His phallus on the rampage was sucked to the hilt; sinking and soaking, it began to hammer. He came, his lust erupting violently. It was over. All that remained were spiders' legs protruding eerily from her scalp, sparse pubic hair in tight wiry crinkles, the smell of blotchy brown skin, the aftermath of cigarette smoke which haunted their clothes, the beer on his breath, his strained red eyes, he flaccid and white, drained of all feeling.

'How are you going home?' he inquired.

'Sometime I charter one taxi, but is too costly,' she explained.

'But I gave you money,' he said, vaguely looking towards his wallet and remembering he had given her his last notes.

Perhaps she misunderstood his expression, because she ripped off the wig she was donning, snatched the dollar bills from inside it and screeched, 'That all I got! Now you say I done t'ief you.'

'No ... no. I know.'

He tried to reassure her, to mollify her. He reflected whether he had any reserve cash in his bedside cabinet, discovered another couple of dollars and gave them to her. She took them, stuffed one under her wig and folded the other meticulously into a small plastic purse. Then he unlocked the door as a cockroach took cover.

She offered to kiss him as she left but he had no desire. Nor did he wish to offend her and their faces almost touched before she disappeared down the passage.

He closed the door immediately. As he turned towards the bed with its crumpled bedclothes he wondered what he was doing in Africa. Why were the inspectors about to investigate the circumstances of the death of an expatriate doctor while dozens of Africans had died? Perhaps Nofi's cousin's husband was among them. Who cared? She hardly seemed to. He felt depressed.

Then he collapsed on the bed and fell into a deep sleep.

After sleeping for precisely four hours he woke abruptly, as if disturbed. But there was nothing. He looked at his watch. It was a quarter to six. Even so he felt that he had slept better than usual. Then in a rush he recalled Nofi and became conscious of his semi-erect penis. 'Christ,' he said half aloud, 'I'm an idiot.'

TWO

5

It was dawn as the inspectors with their liaison officer departed for the airport. The air was cool, delectably cool, as the sun edged softly into the still overcast sky. The low light threw fuzzy shadows from the trees, giving the residential suburb a gentle, English aspect. The road from the National Federal Hotel ran through Akapa, which had once been the district where colonial administrators used to reside.

'Beautiful houses, these,' John Peters observed.

General Martin was in the same car. He said, 'You should have seen them in the old days, when they were properly kept and the gardens were immaculate. I lived here once. For a short time. . . .' And his voice trailed off.

John Peters had heard from Brendan Murphy how General Martin had been given command, at an exceptionally early age, of the National Army. Only months after, a *coup d'état* by one of his own senior officers overthrew the regime and the general was asked to leave in humiliating circumstances. It was as if the forward thrust of his powerful ambition then failed him, for his subsequent career had been undistinguished. At that moment he seemed to have lost his dearly held belief in African soldiery and the personal loyalty of his officers. His private life disintegrated too. He became estranged from his wife, and it was said that his son had grown long hair and taken to drugs. But that was rumour. General Martin was not one to speak of such things, even of his loss of faith in Africa, in the loyalty of officers, in parental authority. A man of command, commanding no one, he soldiered on.

They drove past the cemetery.

General Martin glanced at the driver, then spoke discreetly: 'It used to be said that no black man could have land in Akapa until he was dead.'

The capital was coming to life as they passed through the town. Large women swathed in quantities of material moved majestically about the market-place. On their heads they carried bales, at a slight angle, and with the cloth bundled around their hips they resembled human hourglasses. One walked with a sewing-machine perched on her headdress; one balanced peanuts in a glass showcase. Poultry ran loose between them and an occasional pig. There were goats on a lead. And above the calling, the shouting, the general commotion, a cock crowed shrilly.

The convoy carrying the inspectors on their mission worked its way past *Hello Tailors and Sewings, Expert watch repairer* in a corrugated-iron shack, nails in boxes, ropes, old bottles, crates and ever-increasing quantities of people. People everywhere, milling, wandering, gossiping, arguing, working. Head-loads and fanciful head-ties moved like ships in full sail above the crowd. Obstructed by pedestrians and traffic, the cars drove slowly. John Peters studied a woman beside the road. She bent her knees as if performing a complex comportment exercise, positioned a burden carefully, then rose with stately dignity, while a baby's head bobbed on her back.

The traffic continued to thicken. Incessantly horns and hooters pierced the thrusting cough of acceleration, the grinding of gears. Tyres screamed as motor vehicles halted abruptly when a cow or goat meandered into them. Acrimonious yelling followed. Those without machinery to make noises for them bawled abuse at cyclists, motorists and each other.

Early morning drizzle misted the prospect as the inspectors drove up to the dingy airport terminal punctually at 6.45. A loudspeaker crumbled an announcement when they entered the building. It was unintelligible. The announcer repeated his message. This time those listening attentively unscrambled it: passengers for African Airways flight 385 to Umuadan were advised that the flight would now depart at 8.30 a.m. local time.

As soon as the inspectors were gathered in the waiting-room, General Bergström began: 'This surely is attempt to delay JIG.'

'I doubt it,' said General Martin.

'Not much goes according to plan,' Brendan said.

'But if we are waiting for long,' Bergström insisted.

John Peters looked where the walls were pierced by louver windows. He could hear the rain falling more intensely. The louvers themselves were grimy, giving little light. The lever of one was almost off; the screw hung from its socket by a residual thread. General Martin coerced Major Adeboli into tightening it, which he did with a finger-nail.

'I've tightened the screw,' said Jide Adeboli, grinning. 'Somewhere maybe there's another one loose.' Apropos of nothing in particular he added that there had been no space on the flight for pressmen. Then he followed a group of soldiers passing through the waiting room, and as he was vanishing said, 'Where there's a soldier, there's something to eat – or drink.'

'Comforts for the troops,' said Brendan vaguely.

Jide returned some minutes later and stated, 'I've got a warm stomach. Now chase it down with a cancer stick.' And he tapped a Benson and Hedges from a packet.

A few other desultory passengers waited on bench seats, plastic covered, some red, some black. A German, he had to be, was immaculate in a blue suit, striped tie with a gold, textured tie-pin, socks to match his powder-blue eyes with a pattern on the side seam and shoes, pointed Bally and unpolished. He was earnestly writing notes on top of a Samsonite case which he opened and closed with impressive deliberation before and afterwards. His writing, in a tasteful diary with gilt edging, was minute.

'Jees,' said Jide to John Peters after glancing sideways at the German, 'no wonder he wears glasses.' Then: 'He must get his money's worth out of those air-letter forms.' He disappeared once more.

The inspectors waited with a patience derived from army life. To have read a book would somehow have detracted from the earnestness of their task. None spoke except General Bergström, who began to discourse on his encounter with Pastor Jørgensen the night before. 'Very interesting,' he repeated as he looked towards the Polish inspector. 'You know, Pastor Jørgensen is chief of Scandro and a very experienced man in Africa. I am understanding much better situation here. I think National Government will want to prevent us knowing truth of what is happening in Mbonawi, and perhaps that is now ground for this delay.'

The Pole shrugged a shoulder and said, 'Or maybe weather.' The other inspectors knew he had served on the Eastern Front and returned to Poland only after six years' internment in the Soviet Union. That was supposed to explain all.

'We must begin to think what is happening in Mbonawi,' said General Bergström as if to assert his chairman's responsibility, 'and how can we know the truth. Dr Campbell ...' he started, but seeing no one listening he turned instead to look about him.

A woman from another region sat immobile, impassive, watching without the slightest movement of her head. Only her eyes swivelled. Her hands lay folded before her on the shawl that had been draped over her headdress and fell softly across her shoulders and arms. A second woman, in an orange and blue tailored suit of local cloth, wore a fancy wig and coloured glasses. Impatient and restless she wandered to and fro. As she passed close to John Peters he noticed a discreet fan tattoo at the corners of her mouth, like two elegantly patterned shells touching her cheeks. A tall African in a caftan stood haughtily apart, as if to show that he had nothing to do with the conflict in his country. With characteristic swagger a Southerner flowed about in gaudy coarse brocade, the material enveloping him like an ocean, except where his hands and feet protruded from the embroidered tucking like cutlets *en manchette*. He had the gestures of a man addressing the masses. A metallic cord round his neck safeguarded his dark glasses from the effect of every expansive movement. An Englishman, obviously an Englishman from his stride, paced backwards and forwards, his hands in his pockets and an Anya Seton paperback crumpled into his jacket. Another European, American perhaps, with a plastic raincoat beside him, was near-sightedly reading *Time* while he tapped his foot persistently. He picked his nose to pass the time, stopped picking and looked at his watch. It was only just after eight o'clock. A small black girl with spidery pigtails grew restless and began to cry.

Three nuns in modern habit entered. They looked bleached, their skin pallid and unhealthy beside the Africans, their white habits colourless and frumpy. Then the oldest of the three saw the little girl crying and smiled at her. It was a smile of extraordinary sweetness. For whatever reason, the girl stopped crying.

To pass the time John Peters read a notice on a wall by the benches. It was mildewed, browned in places and dirty. In the poor light he had difficulty at first with the fine print, which referred the attention of the public to Section 459A and Section 459B of the criminal code which state that it is an offence to obstruct aircraft and trespass (459B) on an aerodrome. There was nothing on loitering. Next to the notice hung a photograph of the head of state, crudely framed and just visibly out of alignment.

Notices in other parts of the room proclaimed *Passengers Way Out to Aircraft Only*, with an arrow pointing. The larger of these, suspended from a single nail, had tilted so that the arrow jutted straight up into the air. Several neon lights were working. Although one flickered half-heartedly, the neon continued to cast a cold, clinical illumination on the proceedings. A fan stirred busily near *Baggage Claim Area and Exit*, but there were no arrivals. The other fans remained moribund. In the background a radio buzzed, crackled and emitted. Outside, the insects whistled and whined.

Three soldiers strutted importantly through the waiting-room and out of the far end. Everyone watched the door for a sign of movement, but the only door to squeak and bang was the one marked *Gentlemen, Messieurs, Caballeros*.

Time went very slowly.

6

An African entered the waiting-room wearing a raincoat and carrying an umbrella and brief-case. The *Morning Post* was under his arm. He had just reread his boarding pass for the fourth or fifth time when the loudspeaker came to life.

'May I have your attention please? African Airways announce the departure of their Friendship Service to Umuadan. Will passengers please collect their hand luggage and proceed to the aircraft.'

A man in the waiting-room said loudly, 'I thought ours was the only flight this morning.'

The inspectors and some others left. The Englishman muttered, 'It's a-a-a long time since I've seen the plane l-l-leave anywhere near schedule.'

It was raining in earnest as they emerged from the terminal building. The sky was uniformly grey like the tarmac of the runways, except where puddles patchily reflected light. At the edge the airport was fringed in green, the green dissolving gradually as if absorbed into the sky. Only towards the coast was the definition marked by a frieze of palm trees and casuarinas.

'African Airways, in spite of slight delay, welcome you aboard. Our expected flight time to Umuadan is one hour and ten minutes at a height of 15,000 feet. Fasten seat-belts.' Then the amplified voice added, 'If you have any question, please do not hesitate to ask.'

Piped music resumed. The seat-covers looked an especially lurid mustard as the plane gave an extra roar of its engines and lurched forward. The pitch of engine noise rose. The plane waited, as if poised to pounce, then awkwardly, heavily, ambled down the runway. A soft thud against the underbelly informed the inspectors that they were airborne.

The eternal tin roofs glistened everywhere, scattered over the mud amid florid greenery. Then a layer of low cloud was relieved but intermittently by glimpses of green carpet and the engine pitch changed again as the plane reached cruising speed and altitude.

The haughty African in his caftan took his fingers out of his ears. The Englishman placed Anya Seton upside-down on his leg and every so often peered knowledgeably out of a small oval window. The German resumed writing in his diary. The woman with the shawl draped over her headdress sat immediately in front of John Peters. Above the seat-back she appeared to be wearing one of those winged Dutch caps familiar from sixteenth-century paintings.

The flight attendant announced, 'Ladies and gentlemen, you may now unfasten your seat-belts. We recommend, however, for your own safety and comfort that when seated you keep your seat-belts loosely fastened. Refreshments will be served shortly.' Flight ritual: the common experience of modern man and transience itself, encapsulated with people unlikely ever to be encountered again, traversing time zones, crossing continents, and sharing the prospect, improbable though it might be, of sudden death.

The piped music broke in for a moment: 'Swinging Safari' crackled and ceased in mid-tune. Afterwards there was only engine noise and a loud sibilant conversation loaded with flat a's. Small fans whirred above the luggage-rack, advertising GEC and emphasizing the heat. The air-jet refused to function in any position.

Later there was the rattle of storage boxes being opened and shut and bashed into each other, the tap of plastic on plastic and occasional clink of crockery. The steward began to weave his way through with trays supporting smaller green plastic trays with three Cellophane packaged sandwiches on each: one with a modest slice of cheese, one with a slice of egg and one coated with a substance resembling smoked salmon. After a decent interval the food was followed by coffee or tea, which the steward pumped fitfully into the green plastic beaker already charged with lumps of sugar. John Peters chose tea. As the steward poured, a steady trickle of liquid reached his trousers. It was hot. And the widening damp patch made it appear that he was wetting himself.

'Oh, sorry, sir, sorry,' the steward exclaimed.

John Peters went to the lavatory in the tail of the aircraft. He wiped his trousers as best he could, then had a good pee. It was a pleasant feeling. At that moment an illuminated notice flickered *return to cabin* and minor turbulence rattled the plane. John Peters shook himself, adjusted his clothing, gave his hair a perfunctory comb, tightened the knot of his tie before surveying himself vaguely in the glass. There was a twitch by his left eye. He looked more closely. No mistaking it, a twitch.

The aeroplane was being bounced from one cotton-wool cloud to another as he returned to his seat. He was still conscious of the twitch. It was an alarming, involuntary act of his body, over which he had no apparent control, no influence even. As something not part of himself he endeavoured to observe it clinically, dispassionately. He was over-tired, of course. This was no longer an object of his will, a product of his making, his own doing. It was other and alien. The twitch of life, living like a chicken whose neck has been wrung. All of a sudden it struck him that the twitch was in control, the tail wagging the dog. That appealed; he had become the appendix of a twitch. And in more ways than one. His preoccupation conferred further power, leaving him at the mercy of a nerve. What happens when other nerves begin to twitch? He would become that tremulous, infirm 'old man of fifty', to use Bola's words. He would not even be able to enjoy peeing. Not more than fifteen years to go, he thought. He was half-way to old age, as close in time to fifty as he was to the young man first entering university. Yet that seemed only yesterday.

He had been so full of ideals. And unwilling to compromise. During his last university year the options seemed vast, all was possible, and he had wanted to do great things. To himself and in his most intimate self-revelations he admitted to wanting to change the world. But like so many of his generation he had failed to find a cause in which he could wholeheartedly and unreservedly believe. There remained no masthead of faith to which he could affix his banner and commit his honour. He could find no foundation of absolute truth on which to build the convictions of a lifetime. If only, he thought, he had had creative talent. Had he been able to write or to paint or even to play an instrument well, he might have had that star to follow. That would have given him a compass bearing. But he had not. Academically his record was good, well above average, which served only to multiply his options. Having failed to discern a land beyond the ocean that would be his to discover, he set sail instead on his first voyage of mild compromise. It had been the compromise of doing something useful to satisfy his youthful volunteerism. He had taken a temporary job aiding refugees in Asia.

There had been other reasons as well. There always are. He had been in love. A young, utterly happy and at times hopelessly miserable love affair which dominated his existence for over a year. It aborted finally when the girl he loved wanted so much to marry and he felt unable to commit himself. Yet he couldn't bring himself to reject her, and the honourable solution had been to take employment where there was no provision for accompanying wives. She had even admired him for his idealism. On an impulse she suggested seeking a nursing job in the same country, but nothing came of it. For a long time he remembered her, expecting subconsciously that one day he would return to marry her. Then after months of

silence he heard from a friend that she had married someone
else. Her letter of explanation, which he was sure she had
sent, never reached him where he was supervising a remote
refugee camp. There had been other women since. He tried to
think of them chronologically, but, curiously, the unnatu-
rally enlarged, glazed eyes of the refugees and their bony
bodies came back to him, forcing themselves into his mind, as
they occasionally did.

His time in refugee work lasted longer than he had orig-
inally envisaged. It also punctured many illusions. He came to
realize that politicians and other policy-makers cared hardly
for their fate. They were human beings, individuals caught up
in larger events which they barely comprehended and on
which they had no influence whatsoever. They became numbers – no wonder he loathed the reduction of people to statistics – and numbers of insignificance. Equally meaningful
had been his contact with those responsible for refugee assistance programmes. They were very good people most of them,
but good like middle-aged clergy, who having failed to convert the world are increasingly concerned with their failure to
make a career.

Afterwards he had taken various assignments in Africa, recently on behalf of the World Organization. He had no illusions left about this posting, which was only superficially
important. Although the organization had been invited by the
National Government to send a representative, there was no
mandate from a legislative organ. Member states were always
reluctant to countenance any involvement in the internal
affairs especially of Third World countries; there were to be
no official reports for formal consideration. It sufficed that his
superiors knew he could be counted upon for an intelligent assessment of the situation and a well-formulated presentation
that few would read attentively.

That was the trouble. In Africa especially he had begun to
find the issues terribly confused. There were too many sides
to every question. It was so hard to determine who was right

and who was wrong. He had come a long way since his youthful search for the grail of absolute truth. Indeed he had become convinced that no such thing existed. And without that belief how could one be a doer? You could hardly be certain that what you were doing was right. He envied Dr Campbell. There was a man who had known the right, the right for him. And he had acted. Luckily for him. And yet. . . .

Decisions implied judgement. And simplistic judgements were dangerous. You escaped from the cell of inaction by adopting a course, but so often the map was inaccurate or incomplete. There had been a case recently. Relief workers had been warned by Government forces not to use a particular route. Already frustrated by the repeated obstacles placed in the way of food distribution and health care for what they considered military ends, a Red Cross team decided to ignore the warning. Their car was blown up on a land-mine, and the two who survived the explosion were then killed in cross-fire. It had been an ambush. The National Government was furious because the relief workers had triggered off a trap set against the Northerners, the relief community protested fiercely because the vehicle had Red Cross markings and so forth. Subsequently it emerged that the health and food distribution centre to which the team was heading had been evacuated for days. There were those who saw as an act of retaliation the raping shortly afterwards of two Catholic lay workers by a section of undisciplined soldiers. No logical connection, of course. Certainly no justification. But judgement was complex. Instead of committing yourself to a simple code, you settle for little acts that seem right at the moment.

Again he thought of Campbell. We admire committed men. They have a strength of purpose that infuses their lives. This last heroic act of his had given a significance to his life that it might not otherwise have had, as if dye had seeped back into the fabric. And here he was, John Peters, slumped into trying to see all points of view and hoping to justify his own existence by doing from time to time what he felt was right.

He was becoming absurdly introspective. It always happened when he had done something stupid the night before. He tried to put aside his thoughts and began studying the coloured patterns that appeared behind his eyelids. At last he dozed.

He came to only when the engine noise changed pitch. Piped music streamed into the cabin, the twanging electronic sounds that had accompanied a recent film. When John Peters reopened his eyes he was dazzled by an intense white glow from the rectangular window apertures. He shut his eyes immediately, trying to succumb to that state of physical well-being which is unawareness of the body. The twitch had gone, but there was a dryness in his throat when he swallowed. A slight queasiness in his stomach. He felt bloated, as though overstuffed.

The pressure in his ears increased; he swallowed hard and was again conscious of the dryness. His knees were hard against the seat in front and he found it impossible to make himself comfortable.

The loudspeaker crackled, the music ceased and a steward spoke: 'Ladies and gentlemen, may I have your attention, please? I'm sorry to announce that due to bad weather over Umuadan, we shan't be able to arrive on the scheduled time.'

The music resumed, now jollier, harmonica Swedish style, then a rhythmic interpretation of 'I Gave My Love a Cherry', which petered out while the plane remained in a holding pattern.

'Guess we'll land fifty yards down the road and taxi in,' said Colonel Brendan, who had woken at last.

Every few seconds the aircraft tilted as they continued to circle. The engine droned unabated, abrasive like the white glare from the windows. John Peters stretched his legs across the aisle and tried to rest. But a steward passed, pointedly elevating his feet as if they were the hoofs of a circus horse, and Peters withdrew. He lapsed into a bored doze and contemplated various imaginary faces, and real ones.

He had just focused mentally on an image of Bola and her body when the steward's voice again broke through on the loudspeaker: 'Ladies and gentlemen, may I have your attention, please? In a few moments we shall be landing at Umuadan airport. Please return to your seats and remain seated until the aircraft has come to a complete stop, your seat-belts fastened, and extinguish your cigarettes and no smoking until you are inside the terminal building. Onward bookings should be reconfirmed. I wish to remind those passengers with photographic apparatus that it is an offence against military regulations to take any photographs at the airport.'

The steward tailed off and the music began once more. The plane bumped about uncomfortably in the unstable weather. All of a sudden the earth was there: shrubs and mud. The air pressure intensified. There was a jolt and they had landed.

John Peters held his nose, blew hard and cleared his ears. The music seemed to shout at him, in competition with the whining of the engines and rumble of wheels. Umuadan looked green and fresh after rain, although the sky stayed overcast and gloomy. There was a clatter of seat-belts being unfastened and the music stopped.

Outside, off the tarmac strip, a wounded helicopter had been ineffectively covered, not unlike the work of fashionable sculptors who package buildings. Under a loose shroud, casually roped, Red Cross markings were just visible, and minor damage to the fuselage. A wheel-strut had snapped and the helicopter lay unevenly like an animal with a broken limb.

'That's the relief chopper which, as the National Government says, "ran out of fuel" on its way north,' Brendan Murphy explained to General Bergström.

Umuadan airport terminal was much as the other: a low building with a long-necked control tower near the middle resembling an ornament on the headdress of an Ife bronze. Inside, a profusion of tatty posters advertised the national airline. A stand of pocket-books, which seemed second-hand, completed the furnishings. On one wall two doors bore notices, reading respectively *Gentlemen Maza* and *Ladies Mata*. Opposite, in a corner, a counter served as bar. A troop of Caucasian folk dancers (someone said they were Caucasians) clustered near the bar. The women were peroxide pale and the men exhibited hirsute chests through open shirts worn knotted at the waist. Both sexes had flat Slav faces with pug noses and soulful eyes.

Colonel Brendan happened to stand near John Peters and whispered loudly, 'Do you know how to tell the bridesmaid at a Slav wedding? ... She's the one with braided hair under her armpits.' He paused. 'Do you know how to tell the bridegroom? ... He's the one with a clean T-shirt.'

John Peters looked to see if the women had hairy legs. However, a party of Africans, voluble and excited, came parading through the area with much rearranging of voluminous robes and blocked his view.

The inspectors were conducted to the VIP room. A European woman sat by herself in one corner. A bearded African was reading in another. It was hot, rather small, and a fan droning like a captive bee on a sultry summer's day contributed to the closed-in feeling. On the door a typewritten sheet proclaimed those entitled to occupy the 'VIP waiting-room'. The list included 'first-class Cheifs [so spelled] and Emirs'; 'Chancellors and Vice-Chancellors of Universities' appeared twice, the second time alongside 'Pro-Chancellors'.

General Martin studied the document intently. 'We're not even listed once,' he said.

'Let's add "JIG",' suggested Colonel Brendan. 'That'd fox them. Think we were something to do with those travelling ballet dancers out there.'

General Martin opened the door. It was fresher and cooler. Outside, on the grass verges of the landing-strip, the Caucasians had meanwhile stripped to their bikini shorts and were indulging in a callisthenic display. The women, having removed all superfluous clothing, sunbathed and giggled. An African in military uniform approached them and spoke.

They appeared to have difficulty in communicating. Then abruptly they gathered themselves, their clothes and belongings together and vanished *en masse* into the terminal building.

Shortly afterwards Major Adeboli appeared and informed the inspectors that the connecting flight to Beningo had been diverted. Major Adeboli disappeared again. Someone said there was a rumour that the plane was taking the Caucasians to another sector of the front, where they were to entertain the troops. An airline official announced that the members of the Joint Inspection Group would be advised soon as to the position.

The woman in the corner spoke. 'Do you know what time goes the airplane to Beningo?' she asked vaguely. Since no one knew the answer, she continued: 'I mean on the paper.' Smiling, she added: 'My name is Mrs Jordan.'

The inspectors presented themselves.

'Have you been waiting long?' asked General Martin, being polite.

'I am here since eight o'clock this morning,' the woman replied.

General Martin looked at his watch. It was almost afternoon. 'God!' he said. Then: 'Shut your eyes and tell us what pictures there are on the walls.'

She laughed good-naturedly. 'I can say you there's a picture of head of state and Lebanon and the timetable over there.'

Correct. The faded picture poster of an enormous cedar flaunted the legend *Fly African Airways to Lebanon*.

'You haven't started counting the tiles on the floor yet or estimating how many square feet of material there are in the drapes or how many revolutions per minute that fan succeeds in doing?' Martin said. 'Intelligent people always find something to do.'

'You call that intelligent,' she replied, 'counting tiles?'

Whether or not it was due to Mrs Jordan's presence, the confined space, the indefinite waiting, or the sunlight that trickled into the room, the inspectors became more convivial.

General Bergström had embarked earnestly on a conversation with the Polish officer when General Martin suddenly spoke: 'What we need are poker dice. Liar dice is a great game to play when you have to sit around.'

'I'm no good at that,' Brendan Murphy responded. 'I guess I'm just too honest with my clear blue eyes!' At the same moment he noticed a loose thread on his uniform and produced from his pocket a penknife that incorporated a miniscule pair of scissors. He severed the thread meticulously.

Mrs Jordan mentioned that she had a loose thread on her coat. It proved awkward to cut, but Colonel Brendan succeeded. The Polish officer, whose discussion with General Bergström had fizzled out, pointed his little finger and asked to have the nail trimmed.

There was a short silence.

Colonel Brendan's face lit and he announced, 'Battleships! Who's going to play?' From his brief-case he produced sheets of paper and offered them round. 'I've no squared paper, but this will do for an emergency.'

General Martin accepted a sheet when the others declined. He and Brendan drew perfunctory lines, aligned their navies and began to play.

'H 6.'

'A miss.'

'B 10.'

'A miss.'

The game continued without incident until 'H 9.'

'J 5.'

'God! I'm sorry but you hit my frigate last time.'

'You just made me waste a shot, didn't you?'

'Take another one.'

Mrs Jordan was fascinated.

The bearded African, forgotten in his corner, continued to sit in silence, but was no longer reading. John Peters tried vaguely to make conversation with him. The man seemed reluctant to talk, although his delicate hands and the four small buttons on his jacket sleeve implied higher education. Then he stated very quietly that he had had medical training at Moscow University. Nothing more. No, he did not wish to be introduced to the inspectors. He was not permitted to speak to anyone, he explained mysteriously without being asked. He lapsed again into silence and a glazed staring into space.

Later he looked around him with an expression of total awareness and total detachment. He seemed to peruse the yellow print on the curtains which read 'superior quality. 6 yards'. The merest suggestion of a smile hovered about his mouth, then he reverted to his book, *Bulgaria: A Survey*. He read sitting well back, holding the page away from him, concentrating but uncommitted. For a moment he appeared relaxed in his silky textured grey suit, evidently tailored for him, his toes turned inwards in clumsy socialist shoes. The mild, intelligent expression of his eyes made it plausible that he was a good doctor whatever his political convictions.

Some time afterwards he left the room, escorted.

'Must be very VIP, that man with the beard,' commented Mrs Jordan.

'From what he said to me I believe he's under detention,' John Peters explained.

'I noticed that when he went to the john, that other chap appeared in the doorway,' said Colonel Brendan.

John Peters entered the *Gents/Maza* and relieved himself on Johnson Fireclay, Stoke-on-Trent. The sparkling urine ran along the yellowed gutter over a soggy fag-end and round four deodorant balls. Assorted insects buzzed and drifted. In a dingy corner a large spider devoured its prey and something else scampered for cover.

Back in the VIP room General Bergström inquired whether there was any news yet about the aircraft.

Colonel Brendan said, 'When the aircraft does come they'll discover that the pilot has already flown six hours and that he isn't allowed to do more flying today.'

'Cassandra,' said General Martin. 'Where the hell is Major Adeboli, anyway?'

As if summoned, he marched in moments later, saluted and grinned.

General Martin took command. 'Well, Jide, what's happening?'

'Spot of engine trouble,' replied Major Adeboli.

'When can we expect to take off?'

'Don't know yet, sir. The engineers are working on the aircraft now.'

'Well, that's something.'

The Swedish inspector, recalling his chairmanship, mumbled that it might be preferable to book alternative means of transport.

'Let's see how the engineers get on first,' General Martin insisted.

The hot air revolved in the wake of the fan. The oppressive pressure-cooker atmosphere generated irritability; the weather made towards another rainstorm.

Colonel Brendan walked in and out of the VIP room.

'Why don't you sit down and relax?' asked General Martin.

'We can't sit here all day, for God's sake.'

General Bergström, who had been listening patiently, spoke with gravity: 'What am I saying? It is not looking good if the journalists make a report out of it,' he said. 'Perhaps they are saying that the Government is trying on purpose to delay the tour of inspectors, to obstacle that we are knowing the truth. They are perhaps suggesting that the Government wants to do this to give more time for a – what is it? – cover-up. Don't you think?'

General Martin said firmly, 'In all honesty, General Bergström, from years of soldiering with Africans, I don't think so. I attribute the delays to logistical inadequacy, just that.'

Instead of his habitual shrug the Polish colonel nodded assent.

Major Adeboli returned and saluted. 'Plane is ready for take-off, sirs.'

There was instant commotion. Mrs Jordan got cheerfully to her feet. The inspectors rose, straightened their uniform, collected their belongings and moved towards the door. The detainee stood outside readied for boarding, his boarding-card prominently displayed by one of two escorts. The escorts, both big men, were in plain clothes, one even wore a trench-coat with somewhat surprising brass buttons. They boarded first. Then Mrs Jordan and the inspectors. There were no other passengers.

Hardly were they in than the traditional liturgy was intoned. It concluded, pontifically, that the taking of photographs was strictly forbidden.

The interdiction inspired John Peters to examine the view to see what anyone might conceivably wish to photograph. He saw only tin roofs, green shrubby trees, the scrub and stretches of mud. The wounded helicopter was out of sight, as were two other aircraft he had noticed earlier in a corner of the airfield.

'Ladies and gentlemen, you may now unfasten your seat-belts if you wish.'

There was a clatter of belt-locks being undone.

Through a filter of light rain the trees all of a sudden seemed very close to John Peters. As suddenly Jide Adeboli in the seat in front buckled down, jack-knifing his body, and clasped his head in both hands. John Peters instinctively braced his legs against the chair back before him and held his head down. Tree-tops rushed past at an angle to the window. Abruptly, jerkily, bumpily, the plane hit the ground. It had just made the edge of the airfield. A gasp sounded throughout the cabin, the escape of many breaths held long and hard.

'Here we are again,' said General Martin in loud relief.

On the ground he turned to Major Adeboli, who had been speaking to the pilot. 'What was wrong?' he asked.

'Too much metal in the oil.'

'WAWA,' said Colonel Brendan jovially as they walked in.

'What did he say?' asked General Bergström.

'West Africa Wins Again,' answered John Peters. 'It's an expression.'

'Who is winning?'

Back in the VIP room, where the fan continued to stir the humid air in circles, a captain of the Government forces awaited the inspectors. He saluted. General Martin returned the salute and inquired cautiously, 'Will they be able to repair the aircraft?'

'I doubt that, sir.'

'How are we going to reach Mbonawi? You realize it is urgent.'

General Bergström stood nodding emphatically.

'Yes, sir. By road,' said the captain.

'How long does that take?'

'At least five hours, sir.'

'When can we leave?'

'Tomorrow, sir.'

'Why can't we leave this afternoon? It's not yet four o'clock. I think we should.'

The other inspectors murmured concurrence, except the Polish colonel who surveyed the scene philosophically.

'Is not possible,' replied the captain. 'Sometimes they ambush us up and down the road.' Then he added: 'The transport is waiting outside. To take you to Resthouse.'

As they left the airport it began to rain heavily.

7

An ostrich greeted the inspectors on their arrival at the Rest-house. It had bare, plucked, unwholesome skin, goose-pimples beneath a whimsical cloak of wispy feathers and nowhere to hide its head. At its gristly feet a goldfish pond contained two crocodiles, one supine upon the other, both immobile. An African servant ran a stick over the teeth of the half-open jaws; it went click, click, click like a roulette-ball coming to rest. The crocodile remained unmoving.

Before the inspectors could install themselves, wash or reflect on the situation, a well-dressed lieutenant-colonel appeared. He saluted smartly and smiled. There was a brief dramatic pause. He then withdrew a knobbly swagger-stick from under one arm and proclaimed 'Welcome'. He beamed, looked round and tapped the swagger-stick on a chair back, saying, 'Shall we sit down, gentlemen?'

The inspectors, who had already been sitting for hours, sat reluctantly.

'We have a programme for you,' announced the lieutenant-colonel, 'and we hope you are comfortable in your quarters.'

General Martin responded as automatic spokesman for the Group. 'Thank you,' he said. 'We are very grateful for the arrangements which you have had to improvise. But you will appreciate that our official concern with the events at Mbon-awi obliges us to make all possible haste. If the reports of the Joint Inspection Group are to have international credibility,

61

they must reflect the circumstances at the time an incident occurs, or very soon after. We must therefore make haste. I believe I speak on behalf of the Group when I say it is our hope that we shall be able to leave early tomorrow morning.'

'Yes, sir,' replied the lieutenant-colonel. 'Meanwhile we have arranged for you a programme.' He half turned to a junior officer, who proceeded to distribute sheets of poor quality paper with a carbon-copied list of engagements. 'Look around town' was followed by 'Region Craft Shop' and 'Meeting with Oba'. The programme had been scheduled to begin at half-past two, which was surprising.

The inspectors were glancing through it when General Martin spoke: 'The time is now 4.40, so I suggest we dispense with the first items on our agenda and proceed at once to the meeting with the Oba which has been arranged for five o'clock.'

'O-ba?' General Bror Bergström mumbled.

John Peters explained discreetly: 'The Oba is the traditional, hereditary, local ruler.'

It poured as the inspectors boarded vehicles provided by the army. A civilian automobile in moderate condition was followed in convoy by a military truck which accommodated all but the three who succeeded in squeezing into the flag car.

The palace of the Oba was surrounded by a high wall and muddy courtyard. The palace itself was of cement with corrugated-iron roofing. There was a narrow, unimposing entrance. The inspectors were ushered through, wet and muddied, by four bare-chested servants wearing a livery of brass ankle bangles. The servants conducted the party to the throne-room, where the Oba was seated majestically in a leather wing chair. He was a grizzled, wizened man whose physical presence, like his official position, seemed to have shrunk from a more imposing past. He toyed with a toothpick and intermittently swatted passing mosquitoes.

While the rain drummed on the roof the inspectors inaudibly greeted the Oba, who sat enveloped in his voluminous apparel and motioned for them to take their places about the room. The chamber, an expansive rectangle, had chairs and benches aligned on two sides. Photographs and framed certificates were displayed unevenly on the walls: HM The Queen, the Royal Family at Balmoral (with corgis), Princess Alexandra, the Oba playing billiards. A vast, low table occupied the central space. On it was an exhibition of tribute, a medley of objects arranged as systematically as in a junk-shop.

The Oba spoke at some length in his own language. He could hardly be heard above the rain. When he had finished, the escorting officer translated succinctly, 'The Oba says you welcome', and sat down.

General Martin, on behalf of the Group, responded loudly, emphasizing how happy the inspectors were for this opportunity to pay their respects to the Oba, although duty summoned them post-haste to Mbonawi. While the circumstances of their work in Africa were not those they would themselves have chosen, they welcomed the chance to see more of this remarkable African country and to meet its people, not least distinguished representatives such as the Oba. Then he presented a bottle of whisky. A bare-chested servant marched forward with the bottle, jangling his anklets, genuflected before the Oba in what resembled a sacramental act, and placed it on the offering-table amid the bric-à-brac.

It seemed the audience was over. But the Oba remained unmoving, a stubborn smile on his shrivelled face, and presently the bare-chested servants returned wheeling a trolley laden with tumblers. The tumblers contained whisky and orangeade. Only when all the inspectors out of courtesy had taken a glass, did the Oba himself accept one – filled with liquid of a different colour. He raised it, looked round and said enthusiastically in English, 'Cheers!'

After that, ingestive noises apart and the continual hammering of rain on the tin roof, the room was silent. For nearly half an hour the inspectors sat sipping the sickly drink, hot and increasingly uncomfortable on the hard seats. There was nothing for them to do but study with wonder the collection of tribute.

For no evident reason the Oba rose. The inspectors rose instantly in response. They nodded or bowed vaguely. The Oba departed by a back door and the inspectors streamed towards the entrance through which they had come, where bare-chested servants made an arch as in an old-fashioned children's game, possibly to check whether they had purloined any souvenirs.

Outside in the courtyard, Martin commented, 'Once there were splendid bronzes all round here.'

'What?' asked General Bergström.

They returned to the Resthouse to wash and change.

The Resthouse dining-room was decorated with Edwardian oleographs. A view of *Les Tuileries* by an obscure pseudo-impressionist showed pedestrians in Paris on a rainy day at the turn of the century. Beside this a notice had been pinned to the wall. It read: *No children's matinée until further notice.* The inspectors studied these with feigned interest while they waited for the commanding officer of First Division (Rear) to appear. His arrival had been announced for seven and the military inspectors were invariably punctual. Instinctively they glanced every so often at the clock in the corner. It stood still at 4.10.

Just before 7.20 a crunch of gravel and screeching of brakes announced the commanding officer, who leapt melodramatically from a doorless jeep, flicked a swagger-stick under his left arm and saluted with gusto. His swagger-stick was a hunting-crop, and his trousers were cut so close as to simulate riding-breeches. His cap had been forced hard down on both sides. 'Gentlemen, I hope you are comfortable,' he said, beaming.

'Yes, thank you,' replied General Martin, and the others muttered assent.

Then very abruptly the commanding officer snapped at the steward, 'Take all 'em crates for other end. Make it all clean here!' He continued to the inspectors: 'We shall be eating local food.'

'Good. I am sure we would all like to try that.'

'Would you like some beer?'

The inspectors nodded.

The commanding officer turned again to the steward, who was beginning to move a crate of empty bottles. Brusquely he shouted, 'Why you no bring 'em beer? And bring 'em quick, boy!'

The steward vanished at once, reappearing seconds later with a tin tray on which he had precariously balanced a number of large bottles of Sun beer.

'Up with the Sun and down the hatch,' said the commanding officer, noisily swallowing his glassful.

The inspectors drank also.

Faltering conversation followed. At one point Brendan Murphy asked, 'What became of Mrs Jordan?'

General Martin relayed the inquiry to the commanding officer, who claimed to have no knowledge of her.

'One European relief personnel done come. Woman,' volunteered a junior officer.

'They come and go. It does not make it easier for us to finish this war,' said the commanding officer.

They discussed the conduct of the war; there had been an air raid.

'They say they use gas and, if anyone hear it, it will be bad for 'im,' interjected the junior officer.

The commanding officer glared at him and he ceased speaking. Then to the steward: 'Why no bring 'em chop?'

Garri was served. A lump with the consistency of dough and an indeterminate taste. It was palatable, just, taken with a large pinch of chili for those with a stomach for hot food. Small hunks of broiled meat were also placed on the table.

'Beef,' announced Major Adeboli, and chewed several chunks with apparent relish.

The beef was unbelievably tough, and stringy shreds

worked their way between the inspectors' teeth and obstin-
ately remained there. The generals exhibited increasingly less
discretion in excavating their mouths with their tongues and
even a finger or two.

'It comes here on the hoof,' explained General Martin.

'It should stay on it,' suggested Colonel Brendan.

After finishing another glob of garri, Jide Adeboli licked his
lips. 'I done chop 'em good,' he said loudly and laughed.

Later, exotic fruit appeared, but among it bananas. All the
inspectors helped themselves to bananas.

When they had finished eating, the commanding officer
spoke: 'I wish to show you something of the town.'

The Swedish inspector, having grasped the meaning, instantly excused himself. 'I don't think that is good,' he said,
explaining that he wished to study some papers. The Polish
officer said quietly to Major Adeboli, 'I am going to have a
sleep. I am too tired, my friend.'

The others were ushered into two dilapidated American
cars, presumably commandeered. It was pleasant out, even if
the springs were broken and the car seats were agonizing to sit
on and dirty. The rain had stopped, the air had freshened, and
the night sky was streaked with strands of filmy cloud.

They drove through the city. All laterite. Red earth roads,
red rammed-earth walls and rusty corrugated iron. They took
a side turning and stopped outside a bar. A large neon light
proclaimed *Olympia Saloon*. A festoon of coloured bulbs
offered the only other illumination of the open area where a
number of Africans sat, sprawled, joked round tables waiting
for the band to begin. The habitual concrete floor, cracked in
places and generally uneven, was being decorated with an assortment of rickety metal folding chairs, painted red and blue
(with a number in prominent yellow on the back of each).
Around and about, strung above on pennant streamers and on
the lop-sided striped awning that defined the bandstand, were
innumerable advertisements for Sun beer: *Up with the Sun,
Sun is sunshine, Sun is gold, Grow with Sun.*

'That's meant to be suggestive too in the local language, puts lead in your pencil,' said Colonel Brendan.

From beyond the enclosure came the croaking of bullfrogs. Subtly orchestrated in differing pitches, the rich bass group was answered by a bank of alto and soprano voices. To this accompaniment a cicada sang solo persistently.

Then drowning all natural music, as abruptly as if a tap had been turned full on, the band began. Bodies moved on to the dance space, an arena and not a floor. They disported themselves to the beat that thundered from loudspeakers in every corner. Men danced, women danced, men and women together. It was often impossible to tell which were coupled: men appeared to dance with men, women with women and again women with men. They gyrated compulsively, thrusting their thighs forwards, their buttocks backwards. In an instant the atmosphere had become totally charged with movement and music. The Africans, dancing, entirely absorbed in mass, rhythmic self-expression, ignored the alien inspectors as they sat on the sidelines, drinking beer, spectators, observing Africa. The moist earth exhaled a pregnant warmth in the cool night air.

'It is difficult to believe there's a war on,' said John Peters during an interval, 'people killing and being killed.'

'For these people there isn't,' said General Martin.

'What do you mean?'

'These people aren't involved. They're miles from the front. And they're a different tribe. Like the man in the caftan we saw standing apart at the airport this morning. They're from different regions.'

'What about the air raid which the commanding officer mentioned in passing?'

'An isolated incident,' said General Martin. 'The Northerners inherited a decrepit Fokker which had been used previously for local, domestic flights, and before anyone realized who or what they were, they dropped a couple of handgrenades out of the cockpit. ... Nothing more,' he added after a pause. 'And I don't think many people even knew about the "air raid", but the Government is using it to drum up resistance.'

The band had begun again. The commanding officer motioned to the inspectors to dance. They shook their heads in polite refusal. The commanding officer made to order more beer. General Martin put his hand over his glass. Then he and the others rose slowly and the party left the Olympia Saloon.

8

The convoy had been programmed to depart at seven in the morning. John Peters appeared punctually; after a moderate night's sleep he had recovered. The generals were already there. They all said 'Good morning' to each other, and waited. By a quarter past there was still no sign of the vehicles.

On the doorstep an African woman played peacefully with her infant daughter. The child was decorated with earrings, rings on all her fingers and several gold bracelets. Apart from the jewellery, she wore only soggy, plastic-covered pants – and a captivating smile. She helped divert the inspectors' attention as they watched her toddle unsteadily, balancing her belly, in the centre of which a lumpy navel rose like the boss of a gong.

General Martin decided to telephone the barracks. He was told that the telephone was out of order.

Day formed lukewarmly about them as they waited. The first trickle of sweat ran down the small of the back and dampened the armpits. The air was loud with insects.

'Do you really like Africa?' General Bergström asked John Peters peremptorily.

'In many ways.'

'I wanted to suggest my wife to come. But now I see I shall not. She is in our apartment in Stockholm, where the leaves are soon turning yellow. I love my country,' he confessed with a gush of emotion, and might have been tempted to eulo-gize further had the transport not arrived.

The commanding officer, accompanied by Major Adeboli, was in the lead car. They saluted the assembled inspectors and added a cheerful 'Good morning'.

'We are ready to leave,' said General Martin.

The inspectors and their belongings were packed into the available vehicles and the convoy moved off.

Before reaching the city limits, the cars came to a halt. There was an excited conversation in a local language between the commanding officer and a soldier. The soldier went run-ning off while the others waited. Beside the road a shack made of mud walls and corrugated iron, rusted and corroded to blend with the rutted red earth, bore the legend *Sunlight Hotel*. A notice read *Call in for your Delicious Food*. Behind the hotel stood an isolated palm tree, as if it were a trade-mark, distinct against the sky.

The soldier returned at the double, spoke to the command-ing officer and the convoy proceeded through the outskirts of Umuadan northwards on the only road to Mbonawi.

This had long been the main artery between the south, the coast, ports for import/export and the produce of the north. Traffic was surprisingly heavy. Broken-down trucks and lorries by the dozen had been abandoned at the roadside, but countless others remained in service: great vintage lorries, trucks of all description and second-hand buses, loaded to the gunwale or carrying human cargo blatantly in excess of the authorized limits. The buses bore mottoes, as did most of the trucks.

To relieve the tedium of the journey (the road ran first through unvarying vegetation), and to distract his mind from the physical discomfort (he stuck to the plastic seat), John Peters assembled the mottoes in his mind. He conjectured that, pieced together like a jigsaw, they would compose a pat-tern of local philosophy. The composition began: 'Nothing Pass God' and 'No Money No Friend'. Then, as they passed lorry after lorry and buses laden with human beings and other less determinable burdens, he added: 'All Roads', 'Nothing Pass God' again, 'Little Drops of Water', 'By Grace of God', 'God is Able', 'Safe Journey', 'Good Mother', 'Endurance', 'Slow and Steady', 'God is Good', 'Live for God', 'Long Life', 'No Event No History', 'Be Normal', 'Take it Easy', 'No Telephone to Heaven', 'No Harm in Trial', 'Destiny is Indelible', 'Money Hard', 'Love All but Trust Few', 'God's Case No Appeal', 'Sea Never Dry' ... but these failed to coalesce into a coherent image and Peters lapsed into landscape watching.

The landscape had eventually begun to change. It was becoming increasingly arid as they drove north away from the hot, humid coastal regions. The vegetation grew more sparsely and was less intensely green. Not unlike parts of southern Europe, John Peters thought. Dry earth replaced the mud and featured rocky outcrops where the shrubby trees had been.

After a time the convoy came to a town. All was ochre. Interminable mud walls at angles to each other and in extension made a maze of alleyways. Only occasional small rectangular openings disrupted the wall surfaces, which had been patted and textured everywhere with hand prints, the builder's autograph. People moved and talked less boisterously. The men wore white, loose-flowing gowns with small, discreetly embroidered caps, though one individual was dressed in astonishing yellow headgear with a length of emerald green material descending from one shoulder. The women had on robes of coloured cloth in the tones of natural dye. Many carried head-loads, and posture contributed to their poise and dignity which was combined with an elusive aura of modesty. Then a young girl appeared, wearing only a skirt, her breasts just coming into bud. From her air of bewilderment, the amazed way she looked about her, she was certainly a visitor from the countryside. Her eyes swelled up as a doe's when she perceived the alien inspectors and their escort. She stood for a moment, transfixed. Then she let out a cry and, like a timid, elusive animal, vanished into the forest of alleyways.

Several vultures, lugubrious and purple-faced, perused the scene from the crest of a crumbling parapet.

The inspectors emerged from the vehicles to stretch their legs.

'Where do we go to see Africa?' asked General Martin, once they were out.

'That's a good question when it's all around you.'

'In the Far East,' said John Peters, 'people used to say, "Look at the cannas." Perhaps we could ask to inspect the cannas.'

'Why don't you?'

Peters obligingly sought out Jide Adeboli. He was preoccupied bartering for fruit at a roadside stall. 'Make you come,' said Adeboli to the impassive stallkeeper.

'I'm beginning to understand English,' John Peters commented.

'This man ear too sharp.' Jide turned smilingly, but also to intimidate the stallkeeper into discretion before strangers. Then they fell again to haggling over the quality of the fruit and the relative number of coins. Jide said, 'Make my eye clear small.'

Negotiations were progressing, but Peters feared to wait for a comprehensive commodity agreement and interrupted to say, 'Jide, the generals want to get on as quickly as possible. But where can we have a pee?'

Behind an unlikely building that announced itself as a coffee shop, they were shown an improvised urinal. Inside the shop a box marked Shelltox Aerosols brimmed with home-made sweets. There were rolls of Trebor mints for sale and coloured plastic wiring, sugar, spirit and oil for lamps, and among the kerosene containers lay two golden mangoes. Old canisters of Three Kings cigarettes served as cash holders.

At the entrance someone cooked in a charred pot over a small fire and goats munched whatever was available. The inspectors declined Major Adeboli's kind offer of a cup of coffee and prepared to return to their cars.

A group of children had assembled to stare. Only a blind man, tapping his way forward, moved through the huddle of foreigners as they forgathered to go.

The day wore on. The landscape softened into parkland. Great trees gave shade where a goatherd dozed while his goats craned at young leaves and the cattle nibbled the spare grass. Egrets perched on the cows picking parasites from their backs, to complete a classical paradigm of pastoral ecology. Near the road a monstrous growth of mould disintegrated suddenly into a thinning cloud of white butterflies. Other butterflies floated among branches like apple blossom and petals drifted like butterflies on the gentle breeze. It was all mysteriously idyllic and remote in time and place.

John Peters's wandering thoughts of Mbonawi were distracted by a poinciana in full flower, every hue of orange peel from warm yellow to vermilion. Beyond the tree a small bird battled with a hawk. The small bird in spirited style fought off the hawk, as a fighter might have harassed an alien bomber. While the hawk circled, it dashed hither and thither, round and about, above and below, noisily spitting threats and fury.

Later they passed a flock of goats, brown, white and brindled, black and dappled, and fine, long-horned cattle moving sedately. A man in a round, bossed straw hat was tilling the fields with a short hoe almost identical in design to one in the prehistoric section of the National Museum.

Brendan Murphy was also looking out of the window when a distant group of figures appeared on the horizon. As if to himself he said, 'How often in Africa have I seen that frieze – black figures silhouetted starkly against the sun, in the sand and at sea. Have you noticed how it renders them impersonal?'

John Peters said, 'But it gives them an enduring, timeless

quality. You could have seen the same a decade ago and in centuries past. And you'll continue to see it in years to come.'

'Africa will go on after this war as it did before. One wonders', Brendan Murphy said, 'how much difference a war or two makes. But when I see the children, those little girls with distended bellies and bulging eyes, then. ...' He stopped.

'Yes.'

As the convoy descended from the plateau to the plains of Mbonawi, parkland succumbed to lusher growth. And the temperature rose. The villages this far from town had so far escaped much intensive fighting; there were few apparent signs of war. Only the traffic: not a single civilian truck, lorry or car was to be seen.

The inspectors passed an improvised airfield. Two military aircraft were parked near a barrack-like building; the control tower appeared deserted.

'I wonder where Beningo is,' John Peters said casually. 'We might have flown here.'

'Maybe that is where we were to have landed,' Colonel Brendan suggested.

'Perhaps air-traffic control was overloaded.'

Beyond the road men and women went about their business. A party of women carried home on their heads pitchers and pails of water.

'They hold themselves superbly,' John Peters said only half aloud.

Brendan Murphy looked out of the window and observed the women. 'You know the story', he said, 'about the African diplomat? ... He was immaculately apparelled for some state occasion in full morning dress, but he had his top hat upside-down on his head with his grey gloves lopped over the brim. Someone at last summoned up enough courage to say "Excuse me, Your Excellency, but that isn't the customary way to wear a top hat, and you ought to put on at least your left glove." To which the ambassador replied in impeccable King's English, "I know perfectly well, old boy, how a topper and gloves should be worn, but I don't happen to be wearing my hat right now, I'm carrying it."'

At that moment the string of vehicles slowed on entering the war-scarred outskirts of Mbonawi. A soldier walked past barefoot but in uniform. He balanced on his head an inverted combat helmet with his jungle boots inside.

9

It was afternoon when the convoy drew up jerkily in front of a large house with an uninhabited air. The escort leapt to the ground. A soldier or two outside the building snapped to attention. There was much shouting of orders. Presently an officer emerged to greet the inspectors as they adjusted their uniforms and assembled near the door.

The commanding officer of number two sector, Colonel Osman, suffered from strabismus, but only in this respect did he resemble a Botticelli beauty. Unlike so many of his countrymen he was physically unimpressive. Later, unkind people were to say of him that his interests in life were two – snooker and tombola. On this occasion, however, and for the duration of his command, he displayed a sense of purpose that impressed the inspectors. He had little small talk. And his speech, when he spoke, came in bursts of great intensity like machine-gun fire.

Hardly had the inspectors been ushered into a room than Colonel Osman was provoked by a question into spluttering, 'This is the first time an African army in our country with African officers is fighting a war. The officers are very young and have a lack of maturity and a lack of experience. Your report doesn't have to pass through me. There is nothing to be ashamed of.'

In the silence afterwards a junior officer offered beer.

General Martin said, 'Perhaps I may speak on behalf of the Group if I suggest that we ask the CO to give us a joint briefing as soon as convenient. I think we should waste as little time as possible, especially since the journey here took rather longer than expected.'

'Now?' asked Colonel Osman.

'If that is convenient to you,' replied General Martin.

'What about your beer?'

'We can drink that later, thank you very much.' Lunch, food, drink, beer had to be irrelevant in the circumstances.

'We were expecting you yesterday,' said Colonel Osman severely.

'Were you not informed of the delay because of transport difficulties? We were to have arrived yesterday, of course, but we were obliged to spend the night at Umuadan. I thought you were sent a signal.'

'I never received one.'

The Group trooped into what had once been the dining-room. The windows were curtained with old army blankets awkwardly hung. One wall carried a large map partially covered by a sheet of coloured material. Several rows of collapsible metal chairs filled the remaining space. There was no other furniture. The inspectors sat down.

Colonel Osman picked up a billiard-cue to use as a pointer, gruffly commanded a soldier to remove part of the material hiding the map, and asked, 'Any questions?'

'Before we ask specifically about the incident, perhaps you could tell us, Colonel, where the activity is at present,' said General Martin.

'You want a copy of operational orders?'

General Martin responded gently. 'Just to gve us a general idea so that we can better grasp the overall campaign context in which the incident occurred.'

'There are two main operational areas,' Colonel Osman explained, and pointed the billiard-cue erratically at different parts of the map.

After waiting an instant for further information, General Martin asked, 'Where is there contact with the enemy?'

'Their right flank is still open.'

Another pause.

'Perhaps, Colonel,' General Martin inquired, 'you would give us an account of the incident which took place three – or was it four – days ago when Mbonawi fell to your forces. According to the information which we have received, a Red Cross doctor was killed and a relief worker was wounded in an assault near the hospital, which was allegedly identified by the Red Cross insignia and flag. You will realize that it is in this connection that we have been asked to come – to establish the facts and thus prevent unfounded rumours from circulating.'

There was a minute's silence. The curtain dropped over the map. Colonel Osman put down his billiard-cue. Then he spoke: 'My boys had orders to capture the town while inflicting minimum damage on the civilian population. Civilians who have not been coerced to join the rebels are asked to remain in their home towns. To take an objective without hurting anyone is impossible.'

The British and Polish inspectors nodded vigorously and the others assented.

'You remember Germany and Japan. But my boys achieved their objective. Very few civilians were harmed and none of those who obeyed instructions and remained indoors out of the contact zone.'

'How many were killed, Colonel?'

'How many dead?' the colonel asked an officer.

'Twelve of our boys and six civilians,' he replied.

'You heard that,' said the colonel, turning to the inspectors.

'How many wounded?' Colonel Murphy inquired.

The Colonel glanced again at the officer and repeated, 'How many wounded?'

The officer answered, 'No figure yet, sir.'

'Do these figures include the Red Cross personnel?' asked John Peters.

'Yes,' said the colonel, and the officer nodded.

General Martin: 'You have the bodies?'

'They are buried already,' explained the colonel. 'In this climate . . .'

'Of course,' General Martin interrupted, 'in the heat.'

'Where are the wounded?' John Peters continued.

'Discharged or receiving attention.'

General Martin spoke again: 'Are you able to give us further details about the death of the Red Cross doctor, Colonel, and the wounding of the relief worker, who, I understand, has been well cared for after the incident?'

Colonel Osman appeared to collect his thoughts. He composed himself, picked up the billiard-cue and, leaning on it, began as though rehearsed: 'One section of rebel troops, we think maybe they included mercenaries, were holding out until last Tuesday. They were holding out on a hill overlooking the hospital. They used the hospital as cover. They were firing at my boys, and my boys could not return the fire. Damage to the hospital, you will see, is from rebel fire. We could not carry out a flanking movement without exposing our boys completely to enemy fire. The only cover was the hospital buildings.'

He waited. Then continued: 'One of my officers, he is very young and has a lack of maturity, but he was ordered to lead the assault. He knew the order not to fire into the hospital. When he saw that in the hospital there were foreign people, he did not know if they were mercenaries, he went forward at great personal risk to his own life to command them to come out so that they would not be in danger from rebel fire. He marched forward alone to the main entrance where he could see the faces of the foreigners. He was of course covered by his men. Some sporadic rebel firing was taking place all the time. Suddenly a European man came rushing out, shouting. My officer told him to be calm and for all the people in the hospital to come out and throw down their arms. All would be safe except mercenaries. The European still waved his arms at my officer and yelled for him to get out of the compound. Then he produced an automatic small arm from a pocket where he had concealed it and pointed it directly at my officer....'

The inspectors registered shock.

General Martin said quickly, 'Did I understand you to say, Colonel, that Dr Campbell was armed and that he pointed his weapon at one of your officers? That is a serious charge and puts the events in a very different perspective.'

There was talk among the other inspectors.

'Gentlemen,' said General Martin, as if commanding their attention, 'I think we must ask Colonel Osman to clarify this most important point.'

Colonel Osman repeated word for word what he had said, using the same intonation to affirm that Dr Campbell had produced an 'automatic small arm' from a pocket where it had been concealed and that he had pointed it at the officer. He continued: 'Seeing this, our boys began firing high to frighten the European. But he turned to the hospital to call out his men and was caught by a bullet from the rebel side. An examination of the body might offer proof.'

'But the body is buried,' said General Martin. 'Perhaps we could have it exhumed.'

'Will you exhume it?' Colonel Osman asked, then continued: 'My boys returned the rebel fire, and in the cross-fire one of the Red Cross workers was wounded. He has received immediate treatment. As soon as they could no longer use the hospital for cover, the rebel troops abandoned their position, leaving two dead.'

'Were they foreign mercenaries by any chance?' asked John Peters.

'No. They do not like to leave foreign mercenaries,' replied the colonel. 'But my boys recovered some papers.'

General Martin spoke: 'Colonel, excuse me, but our official concern is, as you know, with the death of Dr Campbell and the wounding of the Red Cross personnel. You confirm one. Are you able to agree that the hospital compound and premises were clearly marked with Red Cross insignia and that the Red Cross personnel all wore the appropriate badges?'

Colonel Osman answered, 'There was Red Cross flag outside and Red Cross on the building, but the rebels are always using this for cover. Usually they have Europeans in front, and when our boys are obeying orders to spare all civilians including foreigners, the rebel troops shoot them from cover.'

'In this particular assault were any of your men killed or wounded?' inquired General Martin.

The colonel turned to the officer beside him. They conferred. Then he said, 'No, no dead.'

General Martin spoke again very precisely: 'Do you have the revolver with which Dr Campbell is alleged to have threatened your section commander?'

The colonel addressed himself in an African language to the officer. A voluble exchange ensued. 'No,' he then stated, 'it was not recovered.'

'Can you inform me what became of it? It would be most important for us to know.'

Another excited exchange.

'No.'

General Bergström whispered to General Martin so that the others could hear, 'It is not possible. I am not believing that Dr Campbell is carrying a revolver. It is against the Red Cross rules and regulations. Perhaps, if they are not producing any evidence....'

There was an awkward silence.

'Do you have any further questions, gentlemen?' General Martin asked formally of the other inspectors. When none spoke, he said, 'Colonel, thank you for this briefing. We are grateful for the forthright manner in which you have described the unfortunate incident. Had the weapon been recovered, it would have been easier for us to convince others. Without it, we must seek corroboration of the account you have given us. Of course,' he continued, 'we are mostly military

men and we comprehend the difficulties of conducting a
war in which military objectives have to be achieved while
non-combatants are spared the effects of military action.' He
paused. 'We should, I think, like to see the hospital where the
incident occurred and to meet the remaining members of the
Red Cross team. I understand that Dr Campbell's widow,
herself a nurse, is still in Mbonawi.'

'Yes. And I like also to meet prisoners of war,' added General Bergström.

'Yes,' said another.

'Would it be possible for us to visit the hospital now?' asked
General Martin.

'It is too late,' responded the colonel.

In the darkened room it was hard to know the time of day.
A clock said after five.

The colonel continued: 'The rebels are still in the district.
There is still mopping up of cut-off enemy troops going on. I
have to be responsible for your safety. The rebels also have
long-range weapons. I have to be responsible for your safety
while you're with me here.' He concluded: 'I want you all to
go back intact.'

'Tomorrow, then, we shall see the hospital,' said General
Martin, 'but would it be possible to organize a meeting with
the Red Cross people tonight? It is important, not least in the
light of what you have just told us, that we meet them as soon
as possible.'

General Bergström said, 'Yes.'

'Yes, you can speak to them,' replied Colonel Osman. 'I
have arranged it for tonight.'

On the way out Bergström asked Peters rhetorically, 'Do
you believe that story? It is as Pastor Jørgensen warned us.
You remember?'

The inspectors were escorted to their billets: improvised accommodation in abandoned properties. The houses had been
designed for air-conditioning. There was no electricity. It was
stifling inside. Even the inadequate windows admitted more

mosquitoes than air. There was no running water. A bucket of murky-looking liquid had been provided for each inspector, to serve all needs. The beds, dirty and long unused, had been covered with coarse army blankets, one on top of the other. No sheets, no towel. In a corner of his room John Peters exhumed an ancient pillow. It had been stuffed solid. He did not relish the prospect of the blanket's male embrace or look forward to a night without mosquito-nets and without air. He reminded himself to bring back a bottle of beer in which to brush his teeth, and possibly to use for shaving in the morning if it frothed sufficiently.

THREE

10

Shortly before eight, transport arrived to convey the inspectors to the house that served as temporary headquarters for the Red Cross and relief workers remaining in Mbonawi. The inspectors were by then famished and thirsty for anything other than beer. On entering the main reception-room they saw with relief a table laid with plates of sandwiches, teacups and saucers. But first they had to be introduced.

A balding man took the floor. He said, 'I am Mr Larsson of Sweden. After the shooting of Dr Campbell I am in charge at Mbonawi.'

Then he nodded round the room at each relief worker in turn, presenting them by name. One wore a discreet arm bandage. Mrs Jordan was there, to the inspectors' mild surprise. Mrs Campbell was the last to be identified where she sat in a shadowy corner beyond the dimming glow of the only lamp.

Mr Larsson pumped the pressure lamp energetically. In the sudden blaze of light the inspectors circulated, introducing themselves individually, shaking hands. General Bergström and Mr Larsson had an animated conversation in Swedish. John Peters went the rounds. On reaching Mrs Campbell in the far corner, he saw her face for the first time. 'Elizabeth,' he blurted out. 'My God! It's you. What on earth are you doing here?' And as he said this he realized how absurd it was.

She responded simply by saying 'John!' Then paused before

continuing: 'I knew you were in the country. I'd seen your name in the local papers.'

'I had no notion that Mrs Campbell was you,' he said.

'How could you have?'

'I heard you had married a doctor, but I don't think I was ever told his name.'

She said, 'Lots of nurses marry doctors.'

He waited a moment and said, 'I'm terribly sorry about what happened.'

She nodded and looked down. The other inspectors and Red Cross workers were talking.

'How are you?' John Peters asked gently.

'Oh, I'm all right, I think,' Elizabeth Campbell replied.

'What very odd circumstances in which to meet again,' he said. He was embarrassed.

'Yes.'

'I wish I had known, that I had guessed Mrs Campbell might be you.'

'How could you?' Then she said, 'We had better join the Group.'

A nurse was distributing cups of coffee and a man offered sandwiches around. Mr Larsson said loudly, 'After you have had a drink and sandwich we can sit down and talk.'

While they were eating and drinking, General Martin turned to John Peters. 'I see you know Mrs Campbell.'

'Well, I knew her years ago. Before she was married. I hadn't realized for a moment it was her. I never knew her married name. In fact, I haven't seen her since. I was on a university diploma programme in London and she was a student nurse.'

'It must be a ghastly experience for her,' General Martin commented. 'They say she is a remarkable woman. Any children?'

'No idea,' replied John Peters.

When all had finished their coffee and sandwiches, Mr Larsson arranged chairs in a semicircle and invited the inspectors to sit. 'Our people have some work to do,' he said, dismissing his staff with the exception of the man with the bandaged arm, 'but Mr Kramer will remain. He witnessed the shooting of Dr Campbell at first hand and can tell you.'

Mrs Jordan also stayed.

As she was leaving the room Elizabeth Campbell said to John Peters, 'You ought to see one of our relief distribution centres.'

'I should like to very much. When would that be possible?'

'Tomorrow some time,' she replied. 'I have to inspect one at midday. You could come too.'

'I should like that.' Then he added, 'Again, I'm awfully sorry about what happened.'

She nodded. 'Good night,' she said.

The inspectors wished her and the others good night.

Those remaining settled into their chairs as comfortably as the austere conditions permitted.

A moment of silence descended on the room. Then General Martin spoke: 'On behalf of us all, Mr Larsson, I should like to say how grateful we are to you and your collaborators for this hospitable reception tonight and for the opportunity to talk over the unfortunate incident of three days ago. May I also on behalf of our Group express to you our sympathy in the loss of Dr Campbell? His was a fine example of the dedication shown by those committed to the ideals of the Red Cross, a dedication which, alas, may even require life itself. Please convey our most sincere condolences to Mrs Campbell. ... Meanwhile,' he continued, 'you who have had extensive experience of humanitarian relief work in times of war know, as we do who have been on active service, that loss of life and loss of limb are facts of life – if I may say so – that cannot be avoided. It is especially deplorable when a non-combatant is killed. We soldiers feel that. More particularly when the non-combatant is devoting himself to the care and recovery of the wounded and sick. Unhappily, such things occur.'

Mr Larsson nodded appreciatively.

General Martin went on: 'It would help us in our inquiries if you were to give us an account, as you remember it, of the incident in which Dr Campbell died and your collaborator was wounded.' He glanced at Kramer. 'We understand that you were all in the hospital compound at the time.'

Mr Larsson waited until he had the undivided attention of all. Then he began: 'It is pleasure for me, not to speak about the killing of Dr Campbell, our much esteemed team leader, our colleague, inspiration, and our friend, but to have this opportunity to tell the International Inspector Group and world opinion the true facts. Our responsibility is for the civilian population, especially those who are sick and those who become wounded in the fighting. We help especially the refugees. The northern area is now being so reduced it cannot accommodate more refugees even if they are receiving more relief supplies. Therefore it is our policy to ask the civilian people and families to stay in their place. To give them more confidence, since they believe they will all be killed or starved in camps, we stay with them. Also because then we can control the distribution of relief supplies which otherwise the National Government troops are taking over for themselves. We are all the team staying in the hospital with clear Red Cross markings as required by the convention. A few sick civilians and refugees were with us together. When the National Government forces were advancing, there was much shooting. You know they do not spare the ammunition. Then an officer, I think he was an officer, comes into the compound near the hospital and is shouting and waving his arms. He was certainly drunk. Most of the Government troops are drunk when they are fighting – this is our experience. We could not understand one word he was saying. I think it was not English. Many of the Government officers have no education and cannot speak English. It is different in the north. Dr Campbell was frightened the man would begin to shoot into the hospital, and if he did there would certainly be more shooting from behind. Therefore Dr Campbell decided he should go out and speak to the man, to reason with him. Dr Campbell was entirely alone. He was very strict that no one go with him, and we always follow his command. We could watch from the hospital. He walked out, quite slowly. The officer was all the time shouting and waving his arms. Dr Campbell was for a long time trying to speak to him. He raised his hand a little to make the man stop to listen. Then he turned towards the hospital, I do not know why. Maybe it was because he thought it was hopeless, maybe it was because he thought he would call one of our relief assistants who speaks many dialects to see if he could translate. When Dr Campbell turned round, I heard a shot very close and then I saw that the officer had shot Dr Campbell.'

General Martin asked quietly, 'Can you be sure that it was not a shot from some other direction?'

'I am sure,' replied Mr Larsson, and added: 'After this shooting of Dr Campbell other soldiers started firing too. There was shooting everywhere from the Government side.'

'Only from the Government side? No cross-fire?' General Martin inquired.

'Yes, there was wild shooting. These soldiers, drunken, were shooting everywhere and coming into the compound. This was when the other was wounded. One of the team tried to get out to help Dr Campbell who was lying on the ground.'

They all looked at Kramer who remained impassive. Then he said, 'That is right. But I am having only a scratch.'

Larsson continued: 'All the soldiers were coming to the hospital, shooting their guns. I did not know what would happen. The civilians were screaming, some of them. Then, quite unexpected, another Government officer came and began to give orders. He saved the situation. He took control. He was very efficient man, not drunk at all, and he was helpful also to the wounded colleague. He came to me and spoke English.'

General Martin thanked Mr Larsson sincerely for his full description of the incident. 'But do you mind', he said, 'if we

ask for clarification of certain points arising from the accounts
of the incident that we have heard so far?'

'Naturally,' said Larsson.

'Is it possible that Dr Campbell had a revolver, as we have
been told?'

'No, certainly not.' Larsson was vehement in his reply. 'It
would be against our rules and regulations. And he was always
very strict about the Red Cross rules.'

'Thank you.'

General Martin turned to the Group. Bergström nodded to
Peters, 'I said this.'

'Any other questions, gentlemen, that you consider it
necessary to put to Mr Larsson and his colleagues before we
leave them in peace for some well-earned rest?'

'I am still having work to do tonight,' said Larsson.

John Peters asked cautiously, 'You're absolutely sure about
the weapon? After all, there have been incidents where even a
relief worker might consider a revolver justified, if only as a
deterrent to protect the women on his staff.'

Larsson became almost histrionic in his reply. He denied
categorically that a man such as Dr Campbell might have been
armed.

Colonel Murphy, as if to change the subject, inquired
whether there had been any sign of mercenaries.

'With the Northerners? Certainly not. With the Government forces? I did not myself see any,' said Larsson.

After that the meeting ended. They all thanked each other
and said 'Good night'. Mr Larsson wished General Bergström a good tour in Swedish.

When the inspectors emerged from the dingy building into the
cool night air, they were slightly surprised to find Colonel
Osman waiting. In the poor light his birdlike physique and
wall-eyed expression made him look shifty.

On the way back to the billets Peters found himself in

Colonel Osman's car. After a period of silence, he inquired,
'Would it be possible, Colonel, to visit a relief distribution
centre tomorrow? I gather from the Red Cross people that
they are continuing to provide relief supplies to the civilian
populations who have remained in their village areas after the
recent advance. This could be a good point to mention in our
report. You know how often the chief minister has stressed
that civilians should remain where they are and that they will
be well treated by loyal Government troops.'

'Certainly. If there is time. But there is always too much
danger of an ambush,' replied the colonel, 'and your security
is my responsibility.' He reflected a moment before continuing: 'These Red Cross, why do they help the rebels? They do
not help our country. They want to weaken it, to break it up.
A united country is too strong for them. They could not
dominate it. They want our raw materials at their price. Our
minerals! All these foreigners who come here treat us as if we
are monkeys. Why cannot Africans fight war without all the
newspapers in America, in Britain, in France saying it is genocide? What of your wars – your bombings, your concentration camps? Only we are black men.'

Colonel Osman went on: 'The National Government did
not invent economic blockade as instrument of war, it is as old
as history itself. You forget I attended your military academy.
I have the same education as your officers. But I am African.
You see, we're not the same. Not better than you – but no
worse either. We do things differently. We laugh differently,'
he looked round, 'and too much, you think. And we cry for
different reasons sometimes.'

John Peters said mildly, 'Why should you be like us? We're
not all that worth imitating.'

'No reason,' said the colonel. 'And no reason why not, if we
want to.' He added: 'We may need your help, but please don't
always tell us what to do. We Africans are too old to be children.' After a moment he continued: 'In this civil war did you
know the chief minister has decided there will be no campaign

ribbons, no decorations to remind one brother officer that another fought against him during the rebellion? We are not fighting the Northerners as a people. Many Northern officers are my brother officers. I cried when one was killed last week during the advance and I saw his body. We were at school together and together as young subalterns. Do your people care?' Then: 'You came here because one Red Cross man is killed. But I lost twelve of my boys, including two of the best. And they have their families.'

'They are married?' asked Peters.

'All of them,' said the colonel. 'Our people like to marry too much.'

Peters listened attentively as Colonel Osman went on: 'And the Red Cross give humanitarian aid to the rebels to help them. Assistance in foreign exchange is used to purchase arms, not food. We have captured many. We have evidence. And these relief flights, they bring in fuel and radio sets and they are cover to bring in arms and ammunition. Without them the war would be over in one month, maybe six weeks. The aid is used for arms, and for vicious propaganda, it is not for saving life. It would be better for the Northerners if you left us alone. What do the Red Cross bring? They bring fuel, spare parts for vehicles, radios. Do you think that is not useful for the Northerners in keeping up the rebellion? And for them to have communication with foreign countries for their propaganda. These Red Cross people – some of them are spies – even give information against us. And the food supplies go first to the troops. We are very concerned about the distribution of relief in the rebel-held sector.'

As the car approached the abandoned property where the inspectors were to stay, the colonel concluded: 'The food relief is for women and children. It is for them, not for soldiers. And in this rebellion, I tell you, all the men are soldiers. Even sometimes women too, they carry arms. But never mind. We have informed all civilians to stay in their villages on their own land. There are many opportunities for innocent civilians to come out of the rebel-held sector. We are now looking after all the innocent Northerners who have stayed in Mbonawi within the means at our disposal.'

'It would be valuable, then, to see a distribution centre. Do you think it possible?' John Peters asked as he opened the car door.

'If it is not subject to rebel counter-attack.'

'Good night, Colonel. Thank you.'

'Good night,' Colonel Osman said to the inspectors. The others had also arrived. 'I hope the conditions are satisfactory. When there is peace it will be different.'

And he drove off.

At his quarters John Peters retrieved his half-empty bottle of beer. Fortunately, the beer was flat. He brushed his teeth in it, which left a brown taste in his mouth. Then he went to bed.

The hot, airless room hummed with mosquitoes. They droned in and out of earshot. He tried slapping them when they settled on his neck, his cheek, his arm, his legs. This made him even hotter. The buzzing persisted. Occasionally he sensed a bite, followed by the itch that scratching made worse.

After a time of turning and twisting and trying to relax, he drew the second hairy army surplus blanket over his entire body and endeavoured to hibernate with his head tucked under cover. Between intervals of fitful sleep he woke, sweating hot and cold.

11

When Major Adeboli arrived in the morning with the official transport, John Peters greeted him: 'God, the mosquitoes here! I've never experienced anything like it.'

Jide Adeboli grinned and, affecting his African joke accent, said, 'Is a very good thing.'

'Why, for God's sake?'

'It keeps Europeans away!' And he allowed his dialect mimicry to disintegrate into an uproarious belly-laugh before saying, 'Make lullaby. You sleep well?'

'Don't be funny. Did you?'

'No sleep,' he said. 'I didn't go to bed. Sat talking and drinking Hennessy with the CO. We were once platoon commanders in the same regiment.'

'He talked to me on the way back last night. I was impressed.'

'Yes. He done tell me,' Jide said, again using his joke accent. 'He likes you. Some good news, some bad news.'

'He mentioned the casualties to me.'

'One of my boys was killed in the assault. His first section was under my command. They are too many.'

'I'm sorry.'

Then suddenly: 'Have a cancer stick', as he offered John Peters his Benson and Hedges.

'No, thank you, Jide.'

General Martin approached them: 'Good morning,' he said brightly. 'How are you, Jide, and you, John?'

'Slightly feverish,' replied John Peters, smiling.

'Feel the heat less that way,' General Martin replied. 'Bergström has a touch of belly palaver so I gave him something. Often happens in Africa if you aren't used to the climate. I told him so.'

After a perfunctory breakfast the inspectors embarked in convoy for the hospital compound. Three of them travelled in a choking old Chevrolet. According to the driver it had been requisitioned three months earlier from the American consul. They passed a tennis-court. Behind the wire netting it was packed with near-naked men like animals in an overcrowded cage.

'What on earth's that?' Brendan Murphy asked spontaneously.

'Deserters, I'm told,' said General Martin.

The Polish officer looked, shrugged a shoulder and said nothing.

The men were all stripped to the waist. Like wild beasts in a zoo they moved and swayed, purposeless and wild-eyed. They might have been waiting for crumbs of stale bread.

'Nothing. Neither bread nor water for twenty-four hours,' General Martin explained, 'and they bake in the sun all day and stay out uncovered all night.'

'It can't be easy to maintain discipline.'

'Imagine the unemployed, the unemployable, the riff-raff. Give them a rifle and a bottomless bottle of beer. Life is very rosy. Until they find themselves forced to advance against fire. The junior officers are only NCOs commissioned at the outbreak of hostilities. It's remarkable that the National Government forces have any discipline.' He added: 'At this level there can't be much incentive beyond beer – and shacking up with a local woman.'

At every turning a soldier on point duty saluted impressively. A section of men walking sloppily as the convoy passed snapped into a brisk march and sloped arms.

The Polish officer mumbled something about bread and cir-cuses. 'It's always been the same,' he muttered. 'In two thou-sand years world is not changing. And if no bread, then just circus.' Then he added cryptically, as if for his own benefit, 'Living, that is all.'

The hospital lay on the outskirts of town below a hill covered in dishevelled vegetation. The compound had been planted with ornamental shrubs: hibiscus grew profusely, but the canna lilies lay flowerless, mangled in their beds. Two small craters marked where mortars had exploded in the grounds, and the walls of the building were pock-marked in places from small arms' fire. Many windows had been shat-tered and splinters of glass glistened in the deep monsoon drains.

'Are you able to tell us precisely where the incident took place?'

General Martin put the question to Mr Larsson who, having arrived moments before the inspectors, came forward to greet them. 'Certainly. I can certainly,' he said, and led them to a spot some twenty yards along the path from the main entrance to the hospital. A paving-stone was stained with blood. 'This is where Dr Campbell was shot and died.'

John Peters suspected Larsson was about to make an unLutheran sign of the cross, but instead he gesticulated towards the hospital doorway and added after a solemn pause, 'There the other Red Cross and relief worker was shot and wounded. Fortunately he was not killed. The bullets, as you can see, could only have come from this direction.'

'Could you tell us where the Red Cross insignia were dis-played?'

'Here was the flag.' Mr Larsson pointed to a flagpole lying felled to one side of the path. 'And there was another Red Cross flag hanging from those windows over the porch.'

'Dr Campbell's body has already been buried, I believe,' said General Martin.

'They took it away at once.'

'The wounded man we know was treated correctly?'

'Yes, he is not evacuated,' said Larsson. 'Mr Kramer is staying to work.'

'He told us his wound was relatively superficial.'

'That is saying much,' commented Larsson.

There seemed no merit in asking once again about the weapon. There was no way to determine circumstantially whether Campbell had produced a revolver. So long as the National Government failed to produce the evidence, there were no valid grounds for challenging the adamant denial of the Red Cross representative.

The inspectors examined the hospital building. Rashes of fire that had disfigured the walls and shattered window-panes could not all have come from the same direction, but no clear pattern emerged. Peters, standing near General Bergström, was reminded of 'belly palaver' by a shelf of disused medicine bottles. He asked how Bergström was. As any traveller would, General Martin had automatically diagnosed diarrhoea and prescribed accordingly. But from an oblique remark it seemed General Bergström was constipated. He started repeating in clogged misery, 'It make like cement.'

The encounter with the prisoners of war followed. It proved uninstructive. None claimed to have been involved in fighting around the hospital. One more articulate individual insisted that they, the Northerners, had been ordered to observe scrupulously all Red Cross zones and had always done so. He said no more after this. The accompanying National Government officer remained several paces away, having been asked to stay apart from the inspectors while they interviewed the prisoners.

General Bergström went up to another and declared solemnly, as if on oath, in his precise and lilting intonation, 'I am Swedish officer. You have nothing to fear.'

The man reflected on this an instant before replying simply, 'I am feeling so much hungry.' As if afraid this point had not been taken, he added for emphasis, 'It looks as if breeze may push me down.'

General Bergström asked John Peters what the man meant. Another prisoner interrupted: 'I haven't got blanket.'

The more articulate individual rejoined the Group, charging that the Government nurses did not allow the sick to see a doctor, that they even rejected complaints of sickness. One prisoner, he then maintained, had had his wrists tied for three days and the feeling was only now beginning to return to his fingers. He summoned someone in his own language. A guard outside shouted back. The man called again. The Government officer made to move forwards, but General Martin, politely and firmly, persuaded him not to obstruct the prisoner of war who advanced into the circle to display his wrists, deeply scarred.

When the inspectors turned to leave, another prisoner, who had not previously said a word, blurted out that a National Government officer had seized his watch, his bank passbook and the photographs of his wife and children. Pathetically, he repeated, 'Picture of my pikin, my pikin.'

In the car afterwards Brendan Murphy said, 'Once I saw bodies slung like venison from a pole, tied hand and foot around it. They were hung too like venison and stank to high heaven. The flies settled on their eyes, blank and partly open, and about their lips. They had been reduced to animals, game, meat. ... You know, one of the locals wanted to eat a sliver of flesh to prove these enemies of his subhuman, since he was no cannibal. The bodies became human again when the Intelligence officers produced from their pockets family pictures, letters, including one in childish script, and a prayer-book, I remember, with passages painstakingly underlined.'

General Martin said, 'I was in another part of Africa when the Hutus rose up against the Tutsis. You know them. The Tutsis are very tall and the Hutus used to be their slaves. We saw numerous cadavers with the legs hacked off below the knee. It was the Hutu way of reducing the Tutsis to size.'

12

Outside the commanding officer's establishment a lieutenant stood idly beside two vehicles. Several soldiers loitered nearby, teasing each other, fooling and giggling. When the inspectors arrived the lieutenant smartened up to tell them, 'Sometimes they ambush us up and down. They come behind our lines in civilian clothes. So we ask them to clear out of Mbonawi and villages. We shall not be blamed if we pull down these villages. Orders to the boys to do the best, but cannot blame them if the enemy come in civilian clothes without uniforms. . . .' He tailed off as the colonel's car drew up.

Colonel Osman leaped from his seat, marched crisply towards the inspectors, greeted them correctly and cut short the lieutenant. 'Transport is here,' he announced, 'for three members from your Group to inspect the relief distribution centre. Adhere to warnings, please.'

General Martin said, 'I've seen relief distribution centres and I wish to speak privately to Colonel Osman.'

General Bergström said bravely, 'I am not yet seeing this relief distribution. I am going.'

Brendan Murphy and John Peters nodded to each other and the two moved towards the waiting vehicles. The Polish officer said nothing and remained behind. An escort vehicle with armed soldiers left first and the inspectors in their staff car followed. The soldiers laughed and waved at friends in passing.

Abandoned vehicles bordered the road on the outskirts of

town. Apart from occasional men in uniform there were no
signs of life. Only when they turned into the open road leading away from Mbonawi did they notice a solitary civilian. An
elderly man was pushing his heavily laden bicycle on to the
road. He hesitated when he saw the approaching convoy, then
decided to rush it. He trotted the bicycle across the tarmac as
fast as he could, dropping something on the way. He had just
reached the other side when the army screeched past. The
escort vehicle halted abruptly and the inspectors' driver had to
stand on his brakes.

'What in God's name is going on?' blurted out Colonel
Brendan as he was thrown violently forwards.

The escorting lieutenant meanwhile jumped excitedly from
his car and began bawling at the old man who was with difficulty endeavouring to manoeuvre the overloaded bicycle on
to a farm track. The officer was after him and beat him about
the head and shoulders with his heavy wooden swagger-stick.
The man cringed, cried out, trying to protect himself with his
arms. The bicycle tumbled over into a ditch, spilling bags of
produce in the mud.

'What's all that about?' Brendan Murphy asked.

'He ran across the road ahead of a military convoy,' said
John Peters.

'We didn't have to stop for him. We didn't even have to
slow down.'

'I suppose the lieutenant thinks we might have had to. No,
it's just another exercise in petty power.'

'Poor old bastard.'

'At least he's alive.'

The lieutenant returned to the escort vehicle and the convoy
took off as sharply as it had stopped. The old man in the field,
his body heaving, held his head, and tried to rescue his pos-
sessions.

The countryside beyond Mbonawi was rolling and apparently open. John Peters pondered how the locals could
hide here 'in the bush'. Then studying more closely the tall

elephant grass he realized a man might fail to see another two yards away through that dense screen.

'We are going long, to relief distribution?' General Bergström inquired.

'I'm not sure exactly,' Peters replied, wondering why he was expected to know. 'I think it's about an hour's drive.'

They turned off the main road and entered a copse of low growth. The vehicles had difficulty in negotiating progress past the branches which jutted like animal traps on to the track. The staff car skidded in the mud and stuck; its wheels whirred without gripping, spattering grimy water in all directions. The driver toyed with his gears and the accelerator pedal. The car slithered sideways. Then surprisingly it began to move forwards.

That instant shots rang out. The escort soldiers in the lead vehicle dropped to the ground and pointed their rifles vaguely into the bush. The lieutenant snapped a command. His men to the right fired. He shouted another order and those to his left fired.

Bergström sat up rigid and displayed his JIG armband. 'We must show them who we are and they will stop,' he said.

'Get down, you fool,' Brendan snapped and threw himself forward on to Bergström just before a shot struck the side of the car, shattering the window above Brendan's head.

Two other shots rang out and all was still again.

'Are you all right?' Brendan asked Bergström.

'My arm ...' replied Bergström, trying to disengage it from under Brendan's weight.

'Keep still!'

There was a tear in Brendan's sleeve where the bullet had grazed him.

For a long time nothing happened. Silence but for insect noises.

The lieutenant finally commanded his men back into the escort vehicle. The inspectors surveyed each other. Bergström was visibly shaken, his face white as ashes. 'Thank

you, thank you. I am thanking you with all my heart,' he said
to Brendan.

'Soldier's reflex,' answered Brendan. 'Normal in the circumstances. Sorry if I spoke a bit abruptly.' Then: 'And how
about your arm?'

'Only it is sleeping,'

'Do you want to go back?' Peters inquired.

'No, no,' General Bergström said, adjusting the armband
on his uniform. 'We must go to the relief distribution centre.
It is possible the Red Cross need our help.'

The convoy continued on its way.

Brendan's sleeve was torn but his arm had only been
scratched. He made light of it. To speak of something else, he
said, 'There's no pursuit.'

'Not in this war,' said John Peters as General Bergström
turned to listen. 'In the bush they are all frightened of each
other. This war is fought along roads. No one controls the
country in between. And – have you noticed? – no one fights
at night. They have fighting hours like office hours. . . .'

'A really well-trained, well-disciplined and experienced
jungle warfare force exploiting the advantages of bush cover
and night cover would go through both sides like butter,' said
Colonel Brendan with conviction, pulling down his sleeve.

'Of course.'

'Then why do they not do this?' asked General Bergström.

'There is too much in the war for many. For the soldiers, for
the profiteers, it is no bad thing. And half of the country does
not care one way or the other.'

They passed a village. A sleepy corporal emerged from a hut.
When he saw the military, he pushed aside a woman cooking
over an open fire, and then rushed back in again to reappear
with his rifle, shouting orders. A body of dishevelled men,
part uniformed, assembled scruffily from different places.

The lieutenant shouted. The escort vehicle deposited two
crates of beer and continued.

'Lubrication for the licentious soldier if it isn't comforts,' said Brendan Murphy.

Presently the convoy came to a clearing. Panic seized a crowd of women and children who had been clamouring at the open rear of a truck from which relief supplies were being dispensed. They scattered to the cover of surrounding trees and scrub. A tall, dignified African wearing a Red Cross arm-band motioned for them to return as Mrs Campbell came out from a hut to address the lieutenant. Politely, but decisively, she insisted he keep his men at a distance beyond the edge of the clearing. In the presence of the inspectors he reluctantly opted to comply.

Then Mrs Campbell walked over. 'Good morning,' she said, 'and welcome. Now you can see for yourselves what it is we do. Oh, do you need help?' she added, noticing Brendan Murphy's torn sleeve.

'A plaster would do the trick,' said Brendan, 'if you have one.'

'Of course,' she replied, producing one from the bag she carried. 'But let's just clean the wound.'

'It had better not qualify as a wound,' said Brendan laughing, 'or they'll invalid me home.'

'I heard you were ambushed,' said Mrs Campbell, walking them to where the water was. 'I expect they thought it was a Red Cross convoy with relief supplies which they need. When they heard the Government troops firing, they decided to retire. The Northerners rarely waste ammunition.' She added: 'We could hear shooting from here. And information of this type travels with gunsmoke.'

General Bergström was following the conversation. John Peters felt sorry for him and asked, 'Was that the first time you heard shots fired in anger, General Bergström?'

'Well,' the General paused, 'yes. Really it is.'

Mrs Jordan appeared from somewhere. She had come with the Red Cross party to observe and to assist. It transpired that she represented the head office of a major charitable organization. She addressed John Peters on the gravity of the situation. It was unfortunate, she said, that Scandro was concentrating so much of its aid in the Northern enclave, but Pastor Jørgensen, the head of Scandro, was a powerful man in relief circles and an impressive fund raiser and that had been his decision.

'Yes, I can see,' said John Peters, 'he's very persuasive.'

'You know Pastor Jørgensen already?' asked Mrs Jordan.

'I met him recently at the Norwegian ambassador's,' he replied.

'Ah. You know also the ambassador?' She was interested. He had established credentials acceptable to her.

'Yes,' he said.

'You know why he is here?' she inquired with a mischievous look.

'Because he's a first-class diplomat,' he suggested.

'You would not believe that,' she said, whatever that was meant to mean. Then in a confidential tone she continued: 'I will tell you. He was in foreign service already. Very clever. Then he married a lady who is rich and from one of the best families and he resigns to be banker. In her family's bank. But the poor man. I know him for years. He cannot live like a banker in Oslo so he tries to go back into foreign service. The Government will not take him because he resign. Only after a long time and using all the connections do they say "Yes". And then they send him here because it is not important post for Norway and the life is hard.'

John Peters smiled. 'That explains it,' he said. 'But of course it has unexpectedly become important and he's doing an excellent job.'

'Yes,' she said, 'and he is helping much with the relief work. It is a great work. Everywhere here are people faminating,' she concluded impressively, as if reverting to business.

The children with distended bellies, the scrawny women whose dugs dangled into empty food bowls, and timid old men all eyed the visitors warily. They were reluctant to engage in conversation even when, as sometimes seemed the case, they knew a little English. The tall African and Mrs Campbell had the disorderly situation in hand. Somehow they insured by firm, unobtrusive supervision that each received his due and none had double rations. Squabbling and arguments were frequent. There was much pushing aside and shouting. But eventually the mass of people, having been given their share, began dissolving into the bush.

Mrs Jordan was visibly delighted that relief supplies were reaching those whose need was so obvious and that they were being competently distributed. She expressed satisfaction that the inspectors were showing a humanitarian interest. There had been much criticism of the relief action, suggestions that the wrong supplies were reaching the wrong people, and now the inspectors should help to put the record straight. 'But', announced Mrs Jordan, 'I am always wearing optimist spectacles. Then the sun is shining always. And I shall tell the people at home what my own eyes are seeing. This is wonderful for them. And there is so much for us to doing still.'

The lieutenant stated he had orders to return without delay. General Bergström said that he had seen sufficient. Mrs Jordan was also ready to leave.

Mrs Campbell said, 'I want to look at some of the children before going back. But you carry on.'

John Peters asked whether she would be safe.

With a wry smile she replied, 'I'm considered the brave one here. It's all nonsense, because there is nothing for me to be afraid of. At first, I didn't care much anyway. And now it's a habit.'

'So how do we organize the transport, if Mrs Jordan wants to leave with us?' Colonel Murphy asked.

John Peters stood near Elizabeth Campbell. 'Could I hitch a lift with you? Then Mrs Jordan can have my place in the car.'

'Of course,' said Mrs Campbell.

General Bergström, Colonel Murphy and Mrs Jordan left

in the staff car together with the National Government army escort.

'I feel much safer when there aren't any National Government soldiers around,' said Elizabeth Campbell. 'The Northerners have total respect for the Red Cross, you know.'

'They need the relief supplies.'

'It isn't only that.'

Then Mrs Campbell said, 'I'm going to examine some of the worst cases of malnutrition to see what we can do. Do you wish to come?'

The examination took place in an improvised surgery: an abandoned lean-to.

The tall African approached Mrs Campbell. 'Madame, I am closing now the relief distribution.'

'All right, Felix,' she said, 'you had better get back and load up again for tomorrow.'

'Yes, madame,' he replied and left with a polite nod.

Elizabeth Campbell turned to John Peters. 'He was in graduate school in the States when the Northern rebellion began. He came back to be with his people. He's a Northerner, of course. One of the finest persons I've encountered in a long time, competent and quiet. He doesn't say much....'

The infant she was examining began to cry. It was an awakening. The blank eyes came to life and glistened in the semidarkness of the shelter. This distorted, pathetic creature with its bloated stomach and protruding navel, arms and legs projecting like matchsticks from a lump of modelling clay, was transformed into a human child.

Outside, a small boy having caught an insect and tied a long hair round the thorax, was busy forcing a splinter of wood into the end of its abdomen. 'Airplane,' he said gleefully to John Peters when he looked out.

Elizabeth Campbell had closed her box of medical supplies and was depositing it in the back of the Land-Rover. Two women tried frantically to detain her, but she repeated that there was nothing more she could do. One of the women grabbed her hand and began sobbing. 'I'm sorry. No,' Elizabeth Campbell insisted. She jerked her arm free and walked to the front of the car. 'I think we should go, John.' she said and climbed into the driver's seat.

John Peters entered from the other side. 'You drive yourself?' he asked.

'Yes,' she said, turning the ignition key and starting off at once, 'are you surprised?'

'Everyone seems to have drivers here.'

The women cried after them.

'It's awful leaving these people,' Elizabeth said.

'What was the matter?'

'Her husband was sick at home. She wanted me to come to the village.'

'What was wrong with him?'

'She didn't say. He had probably been wounded in an encounter with National Government troops and the wound has festered. I gave her some antibiotics. When they don't dare come for treatment, that's usually the explanation. They're soldiers.'

'Should you help combatants?'

'God knows,' she said in a louder voice. 'God knows what is right. Reggie always knew what was right. For him and for everyone else. You just do your best. And sometimes it's all so hopeless. I want to help, to do something about the suffering. I don't know whether it's right or wrong helping this one or not helping that one. They're just people, sick, wounded, dying.'

'You don't believe what so many say that life is somehow cheaper in Africa?'

'Of course not. That's rubbish, absolute rubbish. But there is a difference. Dying belongs to daily life. It belongs to the African's experience in a way it doesn't to ours. We've insulated ourselves from death and giving birth. We've deodorized them, talcumed them and taken away the tackiness and discharge which are their most characteristic attributes.'

'Not least in the heat,' he said. Then he added: 'They're closer too to the cycle of birth and death and regeneration. Perhaps this makes it easier for them to see themselves as links in the chain of existence. Growth and decay are everywhere. Look how everything grows, how quickly and in such profusion and how rapidly it is disposed of when it dies.'

She pondered a moment before speaking. 'It is true. Nature wastes nothing.'

He said, 'Have you been in a game reserve?'

'No,' she replied, 'never.'

'The best game parks are in East Africa, although they have some here,' he said. 'The animals live free. Free to live off each other, to maim and to kill according to their fashion. Only provided the ratio of gnus to lions remains stable.' He thought of the foolish-looking gnu he had once seen first maimed then killed by hunting lions. 'We all live in a game reserve and are prey to each other, and in the long run maybe all that matters is that the ratio of gnus to lions should remain stable.'

She gave him an inquiring look. 'That's not a very romantic view,' she said.

'I suppose I've seen too much of the violence in nature and the violence we do to each other. That's nature's law, Elizabeth.'

'Perhaps the people here understand that better,' she said reluctantly. 'It's an acceptance which I sense in them and I respect it.'

For some time afterwards they did not talk. The sleepy corporal paid no attention as they passed the village. His woman continued cooking. Where the ambush had been all was peaceful; the only sound was of insects and a solitary bird. By the roadside in the mud the body of a small animal had been half consumed by carrion feeders. A group of vultures ogled the carcass.

'Behold the vultures,' he said. 'The scavengers are always with you.'

13

She was concentrating on the driving.

After another silence, John Peters asked, 'Are you going back home now?'

'You mean after Reggie's death,' she replied. 'No, I don't think so. I see no reason. On the contrary.'

'You don't have any children?'

'No.'

'And you?' she inquired. 'Did you ever marry?'

'No,' he said.

'Will you be staying here long?'

'I can't say precisely. They sent me for six months, which will be up soon, but these assignments are always variable.'

'You've become very important.'

'Hardly.'

'But you have many postings like this – to trouble spots? It must be interesting to be involved in international issues.'

'In its way,' he said. 'I'm afraid I have little impact on the course of events. I'm not about to change the world.'

She smiled. 'I remember, yes, you were going to change the world.'

'Aren't we all when we're young, very young?'

'Some more than others. I thought you would, in a way.'

'Now I just do my best.'

She half turned to smile at him.

'Much of the time I don't know what to fight for, anyway.

In Africa especially the issues are so complex. I can't see things simply any more. I wish I could. I might make more of a contribution. Like you – and Reggie.' He pronounced the name cautiously as if unsure whether he were authorized to use it. 'You've made a real contribution.'

'You're right about Reggie. He could be very decisive. He had very definite standards and he was always prepared – he liked the Boy Scout motto – to cope with any threat to his self-assurance. There was even a physical streak to his personality which you could see from the way he did violence to fire-wood. I think he believed he could change the world.' Then she added solemnly, 'I don't believe anyone can.'

'But you do. In so many little ways.'

'Very little,' she added.

'These are the decent acts which add up to a good life, surely.'

She said with great intensity, 'It's all I have, John. Much of the time I wonder what it all matters. Then something happens, something small, and everything has meaning.' She paused before continuing. 'You noticed that child with kwashiorkor I was examining before we left?'

'The one that came to life?'

'You saw it?'

'Of course.'

'That's what gives me life to go on. The children. What have they done to deserve this? What happens to them is worse than Reggie's death. Does that sound awful?'

He shook his head for want of knowing how to reply.

They entered Mbonawi by a road unfamiliar to John Peters. 'We came out a different way,' he said.

'Yes,' she said, 'so did I. In fact this is the first time I've driven freely through this part of town.'

They drove through an elegant residential area. Spacious houses stood in well-planned gardens, now abandoned and lifeless.

Elizabeth Campbell said, 'Before the war this was where the

big company executives lived, the expatriates, and the leading local politicians. Then the Northerners' top brass requisitioned it. It was strictly out of bounds to relief workers, to all civilians for that matter, but especially to foreigners. That's why I haven't been here.'

'They didn't stint themselves.'

'Some of the houses are still well maintained, but look at the gardens!' said Elizabeth.

They were driving quite slowly.

'Let's look round,' suggested John Peters.

She parked the Land-Rover in the drive of a pleasant residence. Together they noticed a bed of squashed cannas, trampled underfoot, and to one side a child's tricycle, broken.

'Cannas seem the symbol of culture. I've never seen them in the wild,' John Peters said. Then: 'That probably happened in the rush for property.'

'I thought they locked the doors to prevent looting.'

'They do.'

A window swung open on its hinges.

'Talk about closing the stable door. There's nothing left,' said John Peters as he peered into the empty building. The movers might have been. No furniture remained: only discarded rubbish, odds and ends, scraps of paper. 'I'm going to look,' he said.

'Do you think it wise?'

But he was already in through the window and seconds later he opened the front door with a flourish. 'Do come in, ma'am,' he said to Elizabeth.

They walked, gingerly at first, through the rooms, which echoed their footsteps emptily. Upstairs, even the bathroom fittings had been forcibly removed. John glanced into a bedroom, to see a huge double bed. 'Good God, Elizabeth,' he called, 'look at this. It must have been specially made and was so huge and heavy that the looters left it.'

They went into the room.

'It's a water-bed,' he said in astonishment. He fell back on it. It wobbled, shook and settled around him. 'It's even clean,' he said. 'They've only just stolen the bedspread.'

'I've never tried a water-bed,' Elizabeth said.

'Now's your chance.'

She stood undecided. He leant forward to encourage her. But the movement of the bed surprised him and he took her hand more brusquely than he had intended and she fell awkwardly on to the bed beside him. Both struggled to recover their composure. Then found their bodies touching as they moved about. Their faces came close. There was only a split second's hesitation. Then instinctively, intuitively, as if it were hardly an act of free will, they drew together.

'You don't know how happy I am to see you again, Elizabeth,' he said.

'And I you, John.'

They kissed.

Without speaking, they began to touch each other, demurely at first, then more intensely as they rediscovered the other person once so familiar.

'It's been such a long time,' she said. 'I often thought of you. I kept your picture.'

Then he took her hand in his and kissed it.

She held his hand and looked at it. 'Your hands are beautiful,' she said. 'I had forgotten how beautiful your hands were. And they're strong too, but very gentle.'

He kissed her fingers one by one.

'My hands are rough,' she said, 'they have become rough. You noticed.' Looking at him she smiled a self-deprecating smile. 'But I'm old, I'm thin and I have wrinkles. I'm losing my shape.' She nodded at herself.

'Don't be ridiculous,' he said, 'you're more beautiful than ever. A little trimmer maybe, a little more mature. But more beautiful even than you used to be.'

'You really think so?' she said happily. Then suddenly with a changed expression she thrust herself into his arms and blurted out, 'You were the best thing that happened to me.'

'Give me another kiss,' he said.

They kissed long and deeply and his hands moved tentatively over her body. She sighed as from the depths of her being and cuddled up to him. 'I don't know if this is right or wrong,' she said.

'Who does?' he said.

'You never married?' She repeated the question.

'Not yet,' he said.

'Because of me?' she said. 'No, that's a silly question. Don't answer.'

He kissed her neck. Her skin was soft and white, her hair loose and soft against his cheek.

'I usually have it up,' she said.

'I like it like this,' he said, 'like you used to wear it.'

'It's longer.'

After they kissed again he thought she whispered 'I still love you.' Then: 'I'm not an eighteen-year-old girl any more, you know. I've grown up. Do you want to see my wrinkles?'

'Oh, darling Elizabeth,' he said, burying his face in her hair, cupping her breasts and beginning to kiss her face and neck.

She dropped her hands to the base of his spine and pulled him hard against her. She moved her hands forward. 'I'm doing things to you,' she said.

'Aren't we both?'

'Yes. Do you think it's all right here?' she asked.

'We would be sure to hear a car if anyone came. But aren't you expected back?'

'I'm known as the independent one. Nobody worries about me before curfew. I often stop by one of the rural clinics. There's no rush on that account, but what about you?'

'The inspectors leave each other to their own devices, but they're quite decent. You should meet them.' He paused and looked her straight in the eyes. 'Some other time.'

They smiled long and deeply at each other. Then, tentatively at first, they began to make love, simply and without haste.

Afterwards they lay content in each other's arms looking up at the expanse of ceiling where two geckos flirted. At the moment of copulation they suddenly fell.

John and Elizabeth both burst out laughing.

'It's a good thing we weren't upside-down,' he said.

Then they looked at each other again.

There was an involuntary movement of his penis as the last stiffness waned. 'The serpent slithers back to its nest,' he said to say something, 'or is it only a snake?'

'Snakes,' she said, 'snakes and ladders, which reminds me of when I was a trainee nurse and spent some time in a children's ward. There was a sweet little boy. As he got better we tried to amuse him. He enjoyed games. But every time one of the nurses suggested snakes and ladders he burst into tears and wouldn't stop crying. It was days afterwards that I finally coaxed him into telling me why. "Whenever Mummy and Daddy are going to play snakes and ladders, I have to stay by myself in the kitchen," he said and began crying again.'

They both laughed.

'You never had children,' he said after a pause.

'No.'

'You didn't want them – or your husband didn't?'

'Oh, yes.' She said nothing for several minutes, then as if she had been trying to decide, she asked, 'Shall I tell you?'

'If you want.'

'Do you want to hear?'

'Of course.'

'Most people thought Reggie a cold fish, which wasn't strictly true. He was rigid, very organized, a law and order man. But he felt things very deeply and he desperately wanted children. He was a great one for history – generation following upon generation, sons taking up where their fathers left off. Historical continuity mattered to him. He himself had been an only child. His father died when he was quite young and he had never known family life. He was always talking about some aunt who had five children and what a marvellous family that had been. When I didn't become pregnant during the first year, he couldn't understand it. We both grew quite obsessive about it. I knew how much it meant to him and I began to think that I couldn't conceive and that I was failing him as a wife. So I went to various doctors. First without telling him. Later, when he got angry, I told him. Then Reggie sent me to one of his cronies, who was *the* man in the field, and he put me through one gruesome test after another. It was rather humiliating and I felt miserable. Anyway they couldn't find anything wrong, so they concluded it was all psychological. Reggie insisted it was because I didn't want children.

'You can imagine how I felt. For months it seems I thought of little else. Then one day Reggie came home brighter than usual. He wasn't very communicative and I could see he had something to tell me. I thought it was probably about his work – he was doing some major experiments at the time. Then he announced in a pompous way. "You know Susan?" Of course I knew Susan. She was his surgery receptionist. "She's pregnant." "Oh," I said, "how nice." I was so preoccupied with my problems at the time, I hardly registered. Then he said, "It's my child" as if he were proud of it.

'I was numbed. I hadn't even considered that. "What are we going to do, Reggie?" I said. "Of course I shall have to marry her," he replied in a manner meant to be matter of fact. It was a bombshell for me and I don't know how I remained calm but I did and I said, "Of course."

'Then they discovered it was a false pregnancy, which deflated her – and Reggie, who came crawling back. Having said he would *have* to marry her as if he were acting out of noble self-sacrifice, he saw nothing strange in reverting to me as another duty. But he did agree with me that Susan should leave his surgery, although she and I had become quite friendly meanwhile.

'Nothing could shock me after that. My universe had disintegrated, everything I had believed in and waited for. For a long while I didn't think I would ever want a child, his least of all. Then by chance I discovered he had undergone a series of tests himself and was probably sterile. He never told me and I never mentioned it. After that, we developed a fiction of desiring my pregnancy, but I knew I need do nothing to impede it on the increasingly rare occasions when this might have been necessary.'

'I began to work in earnest. I had always wanted to, but Reggie had insisted that a woman's place was in the home. When I returned to part-time nursing, it seemed to happen naturally and he said nothing. We both worked hard. It used up our energies and our anger.'

He waited a moment, her story finished. Then he asked gently, 'Are you still miserable?'

'No, not really. I have begun to make the best of what I have. Work is very important to me.'

'Is that why you came here?'

'One of the reasons. As I told you, Reggie was a law and order man. He became obsessed by it. Progress was only possible under conditions of law and order – "like the *Pax Romana* and the *Pax Britannica*" was one of his favourite maxims. You needed a strong police force and arms in the hands of disciplined men to control violence. He was ready to set an example. To instil respect for law, the rule of law was the best contribution that the old world had to offer the new. He was appalled by what he witnessed in the West today, in America and Europe, the indiscipline of youth, which he called kotowing to bullies. He thought everything he valued was going to the dogs. He couldn't imagine, he said, growing up in today's society. He had even rationalized his inability to have children.

'Would you want to have children now?' John Peters asked.

'With all this dying, especially the sick and dying children one sees, the misery, I often wonder.'

'Yes.' He halted before continuing abruptly, 'In one sense I don't believe most lives matter a row of pins, but they are all that matters.'

'And they matter equally.'

'I was reading the other day of a Chinese philosopher,' he said. 'I don't see why all wisdom should be attributed to the Chinese, but he was reported as saying that men, like crows, are all equal, but some cows produce more milk and therefore they are worth more.'

'It's only in retrospect you can be sure which produced most milk.' She paused before adding, 'Is that why we're here?'

'Right here?' he laughed. 'Or in Africa?'

'Both.'

She looked at his body. 'You keep yourself very trim,' she said.

'One hundred and forty pounds fetches the best price,' he said.

'Where?' she asked.

'Where "the pounds" or where "the price"?'

'I know where the pounds should be. You forget I'm a professional nurse.'

'When they sold slaves off the coast here, they fattened them to one hundred and forty pounds, which was considered the ideal weight. Then prospective buyers checked them for muscular development and, Bob's your uncle, a deal! They checked the woman's breasts for breeding potential and the children's teeth ...'

'Doesn't it give you goose-pimples, the thought of that inspection.'

'Would you buy me?'

'How much?' He looked at her closely, lovingly. 'You can have me for free.'

'And my breeding potential?' she asked.

He caressed her breasts again and kissed them. 'No more tests.'

'Suppose I'm pregnant,' she said half seriously.

'Is it likely?'

'I told you that I've been doing nothing to prevent it, and it's that time of the month.'

'Good G...'

She interrupted. 'Would you mind?'

'I hadn't thought of it. No. No, I wouldn't mind. I might even like it. What shall we call him?'

'Are you so sure it will be a boy?'

'I'd like a girl,' he said, 'like you.'

'No, I want a boy first.'

'All right.'

'Then what shall I call him? I'll call him John – after you.'

'After everyone. John. Yes, "John", the ultimate anonymous name. Everyman who'll glide unnoticed into the endless countdown of generations.'

'You're becoming philosophical again,' she said and began to stroke him.

14

The crunch of car tyres on the gravel outside, the sudden shingle-twisting as the driver veered towards the house, and a screech of brakes exploded beside them. Elizabeth Campbell had her dress over her head and the zip-fastener fixed while John Peters still fumbled with his trousers. 'Hospital training,' she said and kissed his forehead. She was flushed. But in the tropics, he thought, white women often look cooked. She put on her shoes, patted her hair conventionally, walked out of the room and down the stairs.

Someone from the car was entering by the front door.

'Ah, Mrs Campbell,' said Felix, the tall African. 'I spotted your Land-Rover and came by to see if there was anything you required.'

'No, thank you, Felix,' she said. 'Everything's fine. I decided to peep at one or two houses, since we need more accommodation, and I thought the National Government colonel might be induced to agree. Come and see the kitchen with me and tell me if you think it's adequate.'

They glanced in.

'Quite adequate and quite clean,' commented Felix before asking with genuine concern, 'I don't think it is very safe for you to enter alone into these abandoned properties. The National Government soldiers...'

'But I'm not alone, Felix,' she replied. 'Mr Peters of the Joint Inspection Group is with me.'

John Peters, who had dressed, roughly combed his hair and put in his pocket a handkerchief that he thought might belong to Elizabeth, came down the stairs.

'Good afternoon,' he said.

'Good afternoon,' said Felix.

'I was just telling Felix about the house,' said Elizabeth.

Then no one spoke.

Felix broke the silence. 'Are you returning now, madame? Mr Larsson asked where you had gone.'

'Yes, Felix,' she said.

They closed the front door behind them and climbed into their respective vehicles.

John Peters, beside Elizabeth Campbell, who was again driving, said, 'What sort of man is Larsson?'

'A male nurse,' she replied. 'Does that answer your question?'

'Is he honest?'

'I think so. He isn't intelligent enough to fabricate convincing lies, but he adores being melodramatic. And he's very defensive.'

They passed the hospital compound. A Red Cross flag hung lopsided from a first-floor window.

'He did have a gun, didn't he?' John Peters asked.

'Who?' She was concentrating on the road.

'Reggie. Your husband.'

There was a tense, loaded pause. John Peters wondered whether it would burst in his face. He regretted what he had said on the spur of the moment. It had been on his mind and the place had triggered it off.

Then she became calm. 'Yes,' she said. Staring straight ahead of her she went on in an unmodulated voice, 'Did you know of the case where the two Catholic lay workers were repeatedly raped by a section of National Government soldiers?'

He nodded.

'When Reggie heard of that he ranted and raved about the

National forces' lack of discipline. Then he said to me, "What if they went for you?" And I replied casually, to calm him, "Well, why don't you get a gun?" He was the policeman, after all, the upholder of civilized values. But I never thought he would. Later he used to say, after he heard about another spate of killings by National Government troops, "If those bastards come after us in cold blood, we're not going to be the only ones to cop it." I thought it was pure bravado.

'He admired the Northerners enormously. All the expatriates did. They're fantastic people, intelligent, organized, hard-working, many of them very well educated, dedicated also – Felix is one. Reggie wanted to retreat with them after the fall of Mbonawi, and it was they who insisted. The top leadership begged him to stay at the hospital, to serve the civilian population which had to remain because there is no more food in the north, they said. But I think they thought he might provide a rallying-point for local resistance and a source of information.'

John Peters could not help thinking of Colonel Osman. And then he remembered what Bola had said and as he did so he realized he had not thought of her since setting out for Mbonawi.

'It was only after the shooting', Elizabeth was saying, 'that I knew for certain he did have a gun.' Then after a moment's reflection: 'How did you know?'

'I didn't. I guessed. Of course, Colonel Osman had said it without any shadow of doubt. But he couldn't show the weapon in evidence, so no one fully believed him.'

'Why don't the National Government produce it?' she asked.

'They haven't got it.'

'What do you mean? What happened to it?'

'I suspect the drunken lieutenant, or whoever he was, pocketed it. As a status symbol. Or he may have sold it.'

'Reggie once talked about buying something from a mercenary. It must have been the gun. But I never inquired. We communicated so seldom. What will happen now? Do you know?'

'I don't think anything. The official inquiry is what counts.'

'You're sure?'

'Yes.'

'I can't help feeling it's all my fault.'

'You know that is not true.' He wanted to put out his arm to comfort her, but they were approaching the inspectors' lodging.

Her tone changed. 'Is this where the travelling circus lives?' she asked.

'They call us that?'

'I'll drop you,' she said. 'Will I see you again?'

'I don't know. What's on tonight?' he inquired.

'The Red Cross and relief workers usually assemble every Saturday evening for a social get-together. Do you want to join us?'

'I wouldn't belong exactly, would I – as an acrobat or clown?'

She smiled.

'What about tomorrow morning?' he suggested.

'I'm off early to another distribution centre,' she said simply, adding, 'What time are you leaving?'

'When the transport is ready.'

'When is that likely to be?'

'God knows.'

'So I won't see you again,' she said.

They stood a moment looking tenderly at each other.

'It's been so extraordinary seeing you again, Elizabeth.'

'Please can we keep in touch,' she said.

'Of course we're going to.'

'May I write to you?' she asked.

'Please do.'

'And will you write occasionally? You wrote me marvellous letters once.'

'Did I?' he said. 'Have you still got them?'

'No. I told Reggie early in our marriage and he made me throw them away. I never mentioned the picture.'

'All right, I'll write you some more, but not if you're going to throw them away.'

'Never again.'

Night was falling as they spoke. In minutes the sky had filled with stars and the sliver of a new moon became visible above the tree-line.

He looked up and her eyes followed his. 'Have you noticed', he said, 'how much vaster the heavens seem in Africa and how many more stars there appear to be?'

'Yes, often.'

'We do make ourselves much too important, don't we?'

'We're all we've got,' she said simply.

An army vehicle drew up before the house.

'I ought to be going,' he said.

'So had I,' she said.

'May I kiss you?' he asked.

'Here? Better not.'

So he kissed her demurely on the cheek. She waved goodbye, hopped into the driver's seat and drove away, saying, 'I shall wait for a letter.'

John Peters walked into the house feeling both elated and empty.

General Martin greeted him. 'Hear Bergström and the rest of you had a narrow shave.'

FOUR

15

The inspectors dined, or rather ate, in the house. Soldier servants proffered dishes of unappetizing food and unlimited bottles of lukewarm Sun beer. The mosquitoes diverted attention from the cuisine.

General Martin turned to Brendan Murphy. 'How's the arm?' he asked.

'Nothing that a simple plaster and a spot of antiseptic didn't take care of.'

General Martin made a few observations about ambush tactics. None of the others spoke. General Bergström smiled wanly and concentrated on declining most of the food being offered him.

'We all have tummy trouble here,' said Brendan kindly.

For a time there was no further conversation. Then John Peters asked, 'Did you see Colonel Osman again?'

'Yes. Yes, I did,' replied General Martin.

'Did he have anything to add?'

'Not really.'

Then silence.

As soon as dinner was finished General Bergström announced that he would go to bed early. General Martin asked if he wanted any more medicine, which Bergström refused with exaggerated politeness. The Polish officer made a notional bow and went to his bedroom.

The others remained for a time listening to the night-time cacophony of buzzing, sawing, humming, croaking, when General Martin spoke: 'I asked Colonel Osman whether I might meet the officer who alleged that Dr Campbell drew a weapon to threaten him.'

John Peters and Brendan Murphy looked round with interest.

'Colonel Osman said he had been posted,' continued General Martin, 'and when I asked where, he gave me to understand that the officer had been subject to disciplinary measures, although it wasn't altogether clear on what charge. I did say to Osman that if they were to produce the weapon or supply more details about the officer's conduct it might give a very different slant to our interpretation of events. I said this so as to let him feel I trusted him as a commanding officer.'

'How did he react?'

'Rather brusquely, I'm afraid. Said he'd already told us that they didn't have the weapon and why did I refuse to take his word for it. Which put me in a bind, I must admit. I didn't much like his manner. I explained that we had to base our report on hard facts.'

They remained drinking awhile. Neither the heavy heat nor the prospective sleeping conditions tempted them bedwards.

For John Peters it was another appalling night. Wrapped in hairy army blankets to fend off continuous harassment by hordes of kamikaze mosquitoes, he lay sweating, and fitful sleep when it came was disrupted by cocks practising reveille. Only the remote rumble of shells lobbed from safely behind the opposing lines soothed him. In the early hours his erection rubbed uncomfortably against the irritating cover, interrupting happier thoughts of Elizabeth and an irrational hope that she be pregnant. When at last a distant bugle proclaimed dawn, it came as a relief.

The morning air seemed cool and fresh. John Peters

emerged to find Brendan Murphy already on the terrace of the house. Colonel Brendan ignored the shooting in the distance and mortar explosions beyond the outskirts of town. Instead he announced, prophetically, 'The heat lies in ambush.'

That John Peters had slept badly must have been obvious, for Colonel Brendan smiled an encouraging smile and said, 'Cheer up! Things could be worse.'

'How, for example?'

'Well, it might be raining. Back at the golf club.'

A slight drizzle began as he finished speaking. They laughed.

Some time after breakfast transport arrived to take the inspectors to Divisional Headquarters. On entering they were greeted civilly by Colonel Osman, who said he hoped that the visit had been satisfactory, apologized for the primitive conditions and the lack of social entertainment, and expressed an interest in seeing the official reports in due course. Air transport for the return journey would be available, he added.

The inspectors thanked Colonel Osman and expressed appreciation for the efficient and soldierly manner in which he had conducted the briefing and made arrangements for the tour.

'We shall not, I hope, be bothering you further,' said General Martin.

'When this war is over, I hope you will come,' Colonel Osman replied.

The small convoy of staff cars and escort departed. Colonel Osman saluted and a section of men stood smartly to attention, a young officer bawling out unintelligible orders.

They drove out of town by the route they had come, then veered to the right in the direction of Beningo. Two miles beyond, an extended train of military vehicles lay as dead as an elephants' graveyard. Tankers, transports, armoured personnel carriers and trucks, massacred, butchered, burnt out and abandoned – cadavers, skeletons.

'No wonder they didn't want us arriving this way,' said Colonel Murphy.

'Then why now?'

'I don't think Colonel Osman cares any longer. He has his own peculiar pride,' said John Peters.

'Or perhaps he imagines we'll think it was a Northern convoy,' suggested Colonel Murphy.

'Are you sure it isn't?'

'They don't have that many vehicles to waste. And we'd certainly have heard about it if it had been.' In awe: 'Some ambush.'

Near Beningo they saw the first civilian lorry. It bore the legend *God's time is best*. Coughing and spluttering it struggled on.

They reached an improvised airfield. There was no aircraft in sight. Major Adeboli insisted that the plane would be arriving very shortly.

'Jide, perhaps there is somewhere we could meet while waiting,' General Martin suggested without sounding impatient.

A store-room was made available. There were three chairs, boxes for the rest.

'I thought it might be useful, so as not to waste time, if we compared notes now that we have left Divisional HQ,' began General Martin, calling the meeting to order. The others nodded assent. 'I think it is fairly private here.'

He began at once: 'Perhaps if I try to summarize our findings, gentlemen. Many of the facts are not contested: that the hospital was marked, that troops, who were perhaps somewhat disorderly – hardly surprising in the heat of battle – entered the compound under command of an inexperienced and overexcited junior officer. That there was a communications breakdown between this officer and the Red Cross team. We all know the language problem. Everyone agree?'

No one disagreed.

'Dr Campbell went out to speak to the officer. Then as to the shooting, versions differ. The National Government maintains Campbell produced a weapon and that their men fired in self-defence, a normal, if regrettable, reaction in the circumstances, and Dr Campbell was killed in the cross-fire. The Red Cross people insist that Dr Campbell was unarmed and trying, by gesture and word, to communicate with the soldiers so as to ward off further escalation of combat in the hospital precincts.'

He looked round the store-room and, seeing no objections, continued: 'No hard evidence has been presented to prove that Dr Campbell was armed. For a disciplined medical man and humanitarian it would have been improper. The only formal conclusion I believe we can reach is that Campbell, being nervous at the time, may have gesticulated in such a way as to alarm the troops who could not have known whether or not he carried a gun. And in the heat of battle they overreacted. I was impressed by the account given by both parties of the manner in which the senior officer comported himself after appearing on the scene. And the treatment of the wounded man,' General Martin concluded tersely. He looked about him, seeking signs of agreement. Then: 'I should like a second opinion from one of you gentlemen,' he said, nodding towards the military inspectors. 'Our friend John Peters submits his reports separately, of course,' Martin added when it seemed Peters was about to speak, and to make clear that he, the general, had all the relevant intelligence, 'but I should like to think the rest of us have reached a unanimous verdict. Or feel free to dissent if you have drawn other conclusions from the facts known to us.'

The Polish colonel nodded.

General Bergström began speaking. 'I am very much impressed by the relief workers. They are fine people. I am not believing the story about a revolver. Pastor Jørgensen, director of Scandro, himself told that National Government would delay us and we would not know the facts for ourselves and then they would tell us a story, you see. But now that is not important. That is strange for me to say. But I am learning many things. First, I have to say "thank you" in public to my good colleague, Colonel Murphy.'

Brendan said, 'Just a reflex action.'

'Then I want to place on record what I am seeing of relief work. It is fine work. It is more important even than the Joint Inspector Group, if you forgive me. And they are living all the time in danger of ambush. Now I am seeing for myself the country and the hard way people live here and those poor children with their starving mothers. I believe the National Government is doing nothing to stop the relief work and that is very good. I mean also Colonel Osman is a good soldier and I want to express appreciation for what he was doing to organize our visit – after we arrived in Mbonawi,' he added with emphasis.

'Thank you, General Bergström,' said General Martin. 'We shall certainly put the sense of your statement on record. However, I still need to know whether the rest of you share my assessment of the main incident we were called upon to investigate.'

Brendan Murphy looked about him before speaking, as if reluctant to present himself as spokesman for the others. He began slowly: 'General, this war isn't doing anyone much good – a few war-lords excepted, but it is being fought to defend the integrity of a country, and, as an Irishman, I should be the last to decry that.' General Martin smiled at him. 'Personally, I was impressed by Colonel Osman, as an honest officer. I think others were too. He is the kind of young officer whose reports I would expect to take on trust in the old days.' He waited before continuing: 'But we are not battalion commanders and neither the National Government forces nor anyone else has produced enough evidence to hang a cat. Nothing, in fact. The relief community representative was, as we heard, adamant that Dr Campbell could not have been armed, and, as far as I am aware, none of us knows anything to the contrary. It would do the relief effort no service were we to accept Colonel Osman's contention without other testi-

mony, and any public suggestions that Dr Campbell carried
arms could spark off a nasty controversy to the detriment of
all without furthering the cause of the National Government.
I don't see why we shouldn't be helpful in the circumstances.
Our report needn't get bogged down in detail. I suggest we
state that Dr Campbell was presumed shot by National
Government troops whose officer, in the heat of battle, misin-
terpreted his gestures so as to believe he had drawn a gun.'

'Thank you, a useful formula,' said General Martin. 'Perhaps we should say "while fighting continued around the hospital compound" instead of "the heat of battle".'

'Rather a long-winded statement for me,' Brendan Murphy
continued in a self-deprecatory tone, 'my testament.'

The Polish officer shrugged a shoulder in such a way that it
was unclear whether he was expressing doubt or assenting.
General Martin took it for concurrence. He was summing up:
'... a verdict of not proven, as they say in Scotland, but
heavily weighted towards the assumption that Dr Campbell
was only gesticulating, although the National Government
troops genuinely believed their officer to have been threatened. I think we must register an uncertain verdict as to who
actually fired the shots that killed Dr Campbell and wounded
Kramer. And credit must go to the officer who appeared on
the scene afterwards for his handling of the situation and concern for casualties. Is that agreed, gentlemen? We can work on
the introduction and the precise wording of our communiqué
after we return to the capital. A good bath should purify our
language,' he added, wiping the sweat from his face.

John Peters was embarrassed. He had wanted to speak. But
for General Martin's summary dismissal, he would have told
them at least part of the story. Now he could only think.

The store-room had become increasingly stuffy and hot,
the seats unbearably uncomfortable when Major Adeboli
knocked and entered. Beaming, he said, 'Would you like
some Sun beer, sirs?'

'No, thank you,' said General Bergström.

'Why not?' said Brendan Murphy.

'When is take-off?' asked General Martin.

'Shortly, sir, very soon,' said Major Adeboli.

'But the aircraft hasn't landed yet.'

'Is coming.'

The beer came. It was warm. They drank a little. Then General Martin asked the others whether they had anything further to discuss. The inspectors opted instead to stretch their legs. The rain had stopped.

As they emerged into the sunlight, blinking, a vehicle ground to a halt. A section of men tumbled out and were ordered to attention.

'Church parade,' said Colonel Brendan. 'That's what we were waiting for.'

A second vehicle followed. Wounded men dragged themselves from it one by one. Others were borne to the embarkation area, where they lay moaning. A young lieutenant with the section sauntered over to the wounded. He stood above a man with leg bandages. Suddenly he whipped a heavy swagger-stick from under his arm and struck the soldier's leg twice. The man screamed.

The inspectors, who had been half watching, winced. General Martin said sharply to Major Adeboli, 'What on earth is going on?'

'Malingerer, sir. Testing for malingerers.'

The lieutenant kicked symbolically at one or two wounded but must have been satisfied that they were genuine, for he marched away, saluted Major Adeboli in passing, and sped off.

As he drove out of the airport area another vehicle entered. A stretcher was carried from the back and into a shack.

The plane landed and the stretcher case was cautiously loaded. The inspectors were then invited to board. The space remaining was filled with other wounded, who groaned throughout the journey. The smell of wounds and sweaty clothing permeated the aircraft. But after one false start the flight itself proved uneventful. The inspectors dozed or endeavoured to doze in the crude web seating of a military transport. The stench was nauseating. Major Adeboli removed his shoes, stretched himself and fell loudly asleep with his mouth open.

They landed in Umuadan. The airport terminal remained as they had left it: the same performance – it could have been the same cast. John Peters looked about for the Caucasian dancing troupe. The inspectors were ushered once more to the VIP room. They were there only briefly. A plane for the capital had been refuelled and stood ready for take-off. They left Umuadan without regret, weary and hungry.

It was late afternoon when they arrived in the capital. The inspectors passed quickly through the main terminal building to find cars waiting. As they left the international arrivals zone a huge billboard faced them: an oversize baby grinned and massive lettering proclaimed, WELCOME TO AFRICA, WHERE BABIES ARE HEALTHY AND HAPPY.

On the road into the town other posters importuned them at frequent intervals. One cartoon displayed a gown caught in the rear wheel of a bicycle, dragging the cyclist down in the path of an oncoming car. It had all the drama of primitive realism. The legend read *'Avoid flowing gowns on cycle. This may be you.* The streets around brimmed over with vehicles in any condition, animals, people in clothing of all kinds, on foot and on bicycles, bumping into each other, blustering, shouting and bickering.

By the time the inspectors approached the National Federal it was dark. In the light of the hotel a bougainvillaea bloomed triumphantly above cannas in profusion.

'I don't remember that mass of flowers,' said Colonel Brendan.

'Hm, no,' said General Martin.

Inside the building Major Adeboli saluted and said, 'Goodbye, sirs. Is there anything else?'

'No, thank you, Jide, that will be all,' replied General

Martin, marching off to his room.

'Poor old Jide,' John Peters said in a friendly way. 'I know it isn't always easy. All this top brass to polish.'

'Well,' Jide said, 'I always say "Better late than never".' He beamed. 'I done bring you to this place.' He added: 'Have a cancer stick!' tapping his Benson and Hedges.

'No, thank you. I must go and wash. Good night.'

As John Peters passed the reception desk he saw Brendan Murphy reading a cable, a wretched expression on his face.

'Nothing wrong?' Peters asked cautiously.

'No, no.'

'Family all right?'

'They're all right, oh yes,' Brendan muttered as if to no one in particular. Quickly recovering his habitual composure he addressed himself to John Peters: 'Got me marching orders. It's from my government.'

'What do they say?'

'Going home, that's all.'

'Can't you persuade them to grant you an extension?'

'No. They've already extended me way beyond the normal tour. I've a good friend at the Ministry, friend at court, and he's done all he can already. National Government policy insists that the inspectors rotate to guarantee the credibility of JIG. Otherwise it could be argued that the inspectors are stool-pigeons. Like me.'

'What will you do?'

'Back to the golf club and the bar stools instead.'

'You'll see your family.'

'Yes. I look forward to that.'

Once in his room John Peters knew he should ring Bola, that she would expect to hear from him on his return. But he had too much on his mind, and he had no wish to discuss the party he had missed or the outing to the beach.

Only after he had bathed and dressed did he finally decide to place the call. As so often with local telephones there was no answer – probably a faulty connection or a wrong number.

It was usual to make several attempts. He replaced the receiver.

When another large cockroach scuttled to safety in the dingy crevices behind the bedside table, he let it be.

16

In the morning John Peters started to prepare his report. It was to be cabled to the director-general of the World Organization and had to be appropriately brief. But it was expected to comprise a political dimension lacking in the straightforward narration of events and occasionally simplistic analysis of the military inspectors. The basic findings had, of course, to tally, unless he were prepared to substantiate meticulously his reasons for differing. Hitherto there had been variations only in emphasis.

From the discussion at Beningo airfield he could guess at the wording of the others' report. Years of soldiering had taught them not to question a command or ask the reason for it. They had a mandate. Their mandate was to determine the circumstances of Dr Campbell's death and the wounding of a relief worker. And in their heart of hearts, as soldiers, they recognized that during war people die, and, once the inquiry had shown death as occurring according to certain rules, the case would be closed. That was that.

Suddenly he wanted to cry out *It isn't true!* He would say that there had been an engagement at Mbonawi. Some twelve officers and men of the National forces and civilians also had been killed. There was no knowing what casualties there had been on the other side, but it had to be presumed that the Northerners too had suffered losses. While National forces were

137

fighting to overcome a pocket of intense resistance, an inexperienced officer among them took command of the area surrounding the hospital compound. The Red Cross doctor in
charge of the relief workers, who had taken shelter in the hospital, endeavoured to communicate. This failed and, believing
himself in danger as well as to protect especially the women on
his staff, he produced a weapon that he had kept in readiness
for such an eventuality. National Government troops, seeing
their officer threatened, shot the doctor and wounded a Red
Cross worker. That would be the truth as John Peters saw it.
And it would place Dr Campbell's death in perspective. He
began to write.

As he wrote he realized that he had no indisputable evidence. Elizabeth would not wish to testify. An inquiry would
solve nothing – the weapon would never be found – and in the
process it might damage irreparably the image of the Red
Cross and the relief community. And bring starvation to the
hundreds who depended on their help. It would be his truth
against the truth of the military observers. And what good
could it possibly achieve? Science makes its own laws and then
determines what is true or false according to these laws. Life is
not a science. In this case he knew the truth, he thought. But is
there only one truth? And need it be told when something can
be personally 'truer'? Campbell had met a martyr's death; he
had died heroically for a cause. Elizabeth could rejoice in that.
The Red Cross would be proud of him and the relief effort
would continue unabated. History books of the civil war
might carry one tiny footnote conveying the gist of the military inspectors' report.

He decided to formulate the sequence of events in such a
way as to justify the officer's impression that Campbell was
armed while quoting the Red Cross team leader's categorical
denial. He elaborated on the food distribution programme
and the humanitarian aspects. It was a report that African
governments could accept without loss of dignity and that
Western governments could comprehend, thus not jeopardiz-

ing support for the relief effort. He concluded by giving credit wherever due. He thought of adding as a confidential footnote: 'Was informed in strictest confidence by member of relief team that Dr Campbell did possess weapon. However, her evidence was not repeated or corroborated by others or circumstantially.' Then he crossed out 'her' and wrote 'this'. Finally he decided to leave it out. No one would pay such meticulous attention to his report.

He had nearly finished when the telephone rang. A voice asked after Mr Peters.

'Speaking,' he said.

'This is the Norwegian ambassador's secretary. His Excellency was wondering whether you might be free for dinner. He has just heard that you have returned and apologizes for the short notice. The ambassador would have called himself, but he is detained at the Ministry.'

John Peters heard sounds in the background, another voice.

The secretary said, 'His Excellency has just returned. He will speak to you himself.'

'Mr Peters,' came the ambassador's voice.

'Ambassador.'

'I would have called you personally but I was afraid of being held up at the Ministry this morning and wanted to reach you before you committed yourself elsewhere. Do you think you would be free for dinner tonight?' Before John Peters could respond, and he was about to say "Yes", the ambassador continued: 'Pastor Jørgensen has returned from the north. He had a meeting with Colonel Kidumi. The Northern leader seemed confident they can carry on indefinitely so long as they have support abroad. Jørgensen believes him. But we shouldn't speak of these things on the telephone. Can you come this evening? Pastor Jørgensen is coming – and Mrs Jordan, whom I believe you met in the bush,' he added self-consciously.

'I'm very sorry,' said John Peters, 'but I have an engagement.' At that moment he could not face the thought of another recycling of the circumstances of Dr Campbell's death in Jørgensen's opinionated company.

'I quite understand,' the ambassador replied. 'The notice is very short. I shall be away for a week or two, then we'll organize a dinner, or a luncheon if you prefer. General Bergström has accepted for tonight so he can tell us all about your findings at Mbonawi.'

'Yes.'

'Goodbye,' said the ambassador.

'Goodbye and thank you again for the invitation.'

Almost immediately the telephone rang again.

'Hallo,' he said, wondering who it could be this time.

'Where are you?' It was Bola's voice.

'Here.'

'Why didn't you ring? When did you get back?'

'Last night. I did call, but there was no answer.'

'I was home all the time. You should have tried again.... You don't seem in much of a hurry to see me,' she continued.

'I had to write a report. You know that.'

'What for? These people should stay where they belong. He was a spy, wasn't he? That's what they do to fifth columnists, not only in Africa.'

She seemed to expect no comment from him, so he said, 'Would you like to have lunch? Perhaps we could go down to the sea afterwards. I need some fresh air.'

'I can't do that,' she replied. 'My mother is coming here for lunch.'

'Well, later then?' he said vaguely.

'I don't think you care! You didn't come on Saturday.'

'I wasn't here. It was you who said you were tied up at lunch-time.'

'I told you my mother's coming.' Then she added: 'You didn't even call me. Perhaps this evening I might be free. We'll see.'

'Shall I call you later?'

'That would be nice,' she said and hung up.

'Bitch,' he said to himself. And this time he bashed a vanishing cockroach with his slipper. The second stroke caught it squarely, and from its crisp coating the pulpy innards oozed on to the wall. Afterwards the ants arrived, and when he looked down later all that remained was a single wing, brittle and with a filigree-like beauty.

After lunch, in the white heat of early afternoon, John Peters felt profoundly depressed as he walked slowly towards the sea. In the noise of the sea there was peace. During the week the beaches were deserted by the sophisticated, Westernized, modern Africans who streamed out on Saturdays and Sundays to play and to picnic. Sun-blackened fishermen recovered their ancestral rights as they hauled up boats and sat repairing their nets. No sound rose above the thunder of breakers crashing on the shore and the rattle of shingle turning when the powerful underflow tore back the water. Locals, men, women and children, occasionally wandered over the sands near the fishing village.

Normally, they ignored John Peters as he lay on his side looking out to sea.

Your horizon is as far as you can see, someone had said. No, he was thinking, your horizon is as far as you can imagine. And he watched a distant ship slip below the horizon leaving only a fuzzy smudge where the funnel had been. He rested, dozing, half watching an African girl with long firm legs in the throes of tying, untying and retying a wrap about herself. The wrap unloosened revealed her bright red underwear.

At that moment a young African approached him. He was a good-looking boy wearing a shirt full of sunflowers and, like a stole round his neck, a towel of many colours. The boy sat down on the sand. Then he said, 'Good afternoon, sir.'

John Peters wondered at first what he wanted to sell. But the boy began talking about himself. 'I live there,' he said and nodded towards the village. 'Please to find me some work, sir,' he said abruptly.

Peter explained that he was a visitor and unable to offer employment.

'What place you live?' asked the boy.

'At a hotel,' Peter replied.

'I live this place,' the boy said. 'I am not married. I live with my sister.' When John Peters did not respond, he continued. 'Are you married?'

'No,' said Peters.

'But you are still beautiful.'

John Peters thought he had misheard. He had not been paying full attention to the conversation. 'What?' he asked.

The boy repeated his remark with hesitation, and inquired. 'What do you like to do?'

'To walk, to come to the sea,' John Peters said.

'Do you sometimes bring girl-friend?' the boy asked.

'Sometimes.' He wished to remain, but decided it would be prudent to move and began to put on his socks and shoes, having first shaken out the sand.

'Since you not married,' the boy insisted, 'do you like play with boys or play with girls?'

'Girls.'

The boy appeared hardly to hear.

John Peters, picking up his shirt, inadvertently sprinkled sand over him. 'Sorry, sorry,' he said quickly, and then repeated 'Girls'.

He looked to see what had become of the girl with bright red knickers and left.

Peters passed a woman with peanuts for sale, God knows to whom. On her head she balanced, off-centre, a contraption that contained the nuts, her money-tin and other bric-à-brac. Her hair beneath was drawn taut from patches, plaited as if to divide her head like the segments of a citrus fruit.

They ignored each other.

As he walked home the late afternoon sun cast a haze over

the village, silhouetting a figure and a solitary palm with its toes in the water. The spray from breaking waves floated like a cloud of light above the surface of the sea. In the distance he saw a frieze of fishermen returning with the day's catch.

17

Shortly after sunset John Peters drove to Bola's residence in the elegant part of town known as the Esplanade. He passed the US ambassador's residence with its massive doors of burnished bronze, and, in its colonially genteel garden setting beside the lagoon, the dirty white façade of State House. Then the beautiful mellowed brick of the one-time Secretariat building. Beyond lay the burgeoning capital of post-independence development: skyscrapers, modern office blocks and nondescript modern hotels, which were already beginning to take on the tropical patina of mildew, flaking paint and humid patches.

Not far behind the Esplanade was the bustling African township, full of colour, shouting, slapping, laughter and argument. And litter. Still farther away were the remnants of an even older settlement. Here houses and huts had been raised on stilts over the mud-flats where tidal eddies carried excrement, debris and rubbish of all sorts to and fro. This was a village of nets, fishing-smacks and canoes, and the flotsam and jetsam that accumulate where dry land and ocean meet. As darkness fell it came mysteriously alive with will-o'-the-wisp oil lamps swaying irregularly, fading behind a screen of walls or moving figures, and reflected here and there in puddles and the mirror face of water.

The world of the Esplanade would have been brightly lit in

peacetime. During the civil war with the Northerners, the National Government had decreed a black-out in the streets as much for reasons of austerity as a precaution against the implausible eventuality of an air raid. There were no street lamps to illuminate the cathedral, but its commanding presence dominated the central Esplanade near Bola's apartment. As John Peters left the car he felt the heavy architecture and unmistakable Anglican quality that seemed so alien to Africa and yet so solidly implanted there. In the churchyard giant spreading trees cast eerie shadows.

He turned the corner, entered a building and climbed the stairs. A houseboy answered the bell. Bola came afterwards. In front of servants she was always reserved. She said 'How are you?' and invited him in. The houseboy genuflected before her and was dismissed.

John Peters took Bola to kiss her on the cheek, but she said, 'Wait a minute.'

They sat together in the drawing-room, curiously formal. Bola herself served drinks. 'Well,' she said, 'when is it going to end?'

'God knows.'

'I thought after Mbonawi again, they were finished.'

'I don't have that impression.'

'This relief nonsense. The Red Cross behave like little barons – and it isn't their country. Why can't they leave Africa to the Africans? If only the foreigners didn't interfere.'

'But even the chief minister says he doesn't want a military solution. Of course, it may be a way of justifying the slow progress to date. But I believe him. He's patently sincere. And the Red Cross people, whatever you may say, do a lot of good as well. I saw a relief distribution centre and was quite impressed,' he said, wanting to speak about Elizabeth.

She was uninterested. She said, 'The chief minister's not very brilliant, you know. They just put him there after the last army take-over. And what of the hawks? They run him.'

'I don't know. It's difficult to be sure who takes the decisions and who has the power to implement them when they're taken.'

When she made no comment, he continued. 'Too many people, especially in the army, have a vested interest in continuing the war.'

She exploded angrily but found no words for her fury. Bola was not alone in a certain confusion of loyalties and assessment of the war. In her class there were many like her.

To change the mood, he said, 'I heard a story from the driver this evening. He told me that his brother had asked him in a letter to cable that his wife had died.' It had reminded him of Nofi's cousin at the Rajah Club, but that would be unwise to tell Bola. 'The brother did not actually have a wife, but that was the only way he could obtain leave. According to the driver, "They all say they married, then can collect wife allowance."' Bola failed to appreciate his imitation of the driver's accent. 'I asked whether no one ever checked and he replied, "They no time check." And then he added brightly, "Can marry one more."'

The steward entered and knelt. Bola instructed him to serve and she and John Peters went to the table. There was the minimum of conversation between them during dinner.

After eating she walked directly into her bedroom without a word, and he followed discreetly.

'There's a mosquito in your net,' he said.

'Is there?'

'I'd be jealous to think of it sleeping with you.'

He watched it settle, a black spot on white open-weave netting, a speck of dust, dandruff. Then it flew up, buzzing. He leant forwards, clapped his hands together and caught it.

Bola had been looking in the mirror, swivelled round in alarm, and blurted out, 'Oh, darling!'

He showed her the mosquito, a squiggle of dirty black on his palm.

Irritably she said, 'I don't want to see a dead mosquito.'

'I was just killing it,' he replied.

'Ugh,' she said, 'there's a time and place for everything.'

She stood in the flattering, indirect light of the room, her body repeated in the mirror. She had an astonishing body. Her face was not beautiful, but her breasts, the tenuous waist, her buttocks and thighs were firm, soft, sinuous and shaped to form a tactile whole so sexually provocative that he was pulled towards her as a male animal is chemically drawn to the receptive female.

They embraced. He began to unzip her dress, but then she shook it off herself and stood for a moment in a white bra and panties, which made her ever more desirable before she took these off also and disappeared inside the mosquito-net.

He undressed and followed.

In silence on the bed they were soon moving together.

'Don't come too quickly,' she said coolly, as if quoting from a sex manual.

For him this technical guidance perverted the moment of single-minded passion. And when once more she said 'Darling, don't come yet' it nauseated him. It deflated his desire: she the driving instructress and he the automaton stud, which was what in that moment he realized he had become – and failed to be as he began to go limp. He tried concentrating all his feeling and force, to drive blood into the fuse. He grasped her buttocks and drew her strongly against him.

'Not so hard,' she said, and at that moment the thrust of her pelvis jerking slipped him out, flaccid.

She almost screamed. 'Darling, that's terrible. What happened?'

'I don't know,' he said. 'I don't know.'

'Never mind,' she said like a schoolmistress. 'Lie down and rest.' Then she added: 'Tomorrow I'll have the curse.'

There was a pause. They lay side by side without speaking. He listened to her breath, irregular and hard. 'Do you want to try again?' he asked.

'If you do.'

He became hard enough to enter, but as he floated inside her, he felt the blood ebbing. 'Sometimes you hold me inside,' he said.

'What do you mean?'

'Inside yourself. Perhaps you don't realize when you do it.'

'No.'

She did not react as he expected.

He endeavoured to keep his erection. He tried not to think of it all the time, as though thinking would dissipate the effect like light on a dark spot, or the effort to remember would create that membrane of concentration which memory cannot penetrate. He lay on her, relaxing. He looked around, his eyes not fastening on anything. This had not happened to him before. He thought of Elizabeth. He started to talk of other things. He went limp.

She did not realize it immediately, but when his penis slid out of her again she became angry.

'I'm sorry,' he said. 'I think I'm over-tired.'

'You weren't concentrating,' she said. 'You were looking at things in the room. And then you started talking about this and that. You shouldn't talk when you make love, at least not just normally. You should concentrate if you want to make love to me. ... I'm getting up,' she announced.

She rose from the bed, seemed to shake off a shiver and began to dress. He dressed also. They did not look at each other.

'I'm sorry,' he said, putting an arm round her shoulders.

She moved away from him. 'It doesn't matter,' she said. Then a moment later: 'I must have a cigarette. I haven't had one since lunch.'

He lit her cigarette with her Dunhill lighter and, smiling, said, 'Yes, you have. I could taste it.'

She ignored him and said, 'I'm still hungry. Would you like anything?'

'No, thank you. A drink perhaps. I can get it myself.'

'All right.'

She put a popular disc on the record-player. It was not to his liking, as she knew.

'I'm going to the kitchen. The steward's gone off. I sent him home so we could be alone.'

He made himself a weak whisky and soda and wandered on to the veranda, which overlooked the Esplanade. The light evening wind bore the cool kiss of sea air to his face. A few stars pricked the darkness of the sky, a few distant lights from ships' lanterns bobbed on the dark water. Below him on the Esplanade itself the headlights of passing cars provided intermittent illumination, but for the rest it was black. In the blackness he was conscious of an occasional pedestrian stumbling against the kerb, a cyclist manoeuvring through the night, and muffled figures sleeping in the churchyard precincts that surrounded the confident cathedral mass.

He was watching the lanterns when it happened.

A car came hurtling round the corner of the pitch-dark street and hit someone. The thud resounded and was followed by a stifled scream, the clatter of metal. Seconds' abrupt commotion, concentrated violence. The explosive impact. Then the car drove on and there was nothing to see.

John Peters was sure he heard a man groaning. He made towards the front door.

Bola came in from the kitchen at the same time. 'Where are you going?' she said in astonishment.

'There's been an accident,' he said. 'I happened to see it. There's someone down there. In the middle of the road.'

'What's that to do with you?'

'He's there. He's there in the middle of the road. I can't leave him lying there.'

'Don't be a fool. Anything could happen. It's none of your business.'

'There's a man in the middle of the road. If another car comes, it'll probably go right over him'

'This is Africa. It's none of your business,' she repeated. 'Leave him alone.'

But John Peters walked past her out of the door. He ran down the stairs and into the street.

At first in the darkness he saw nothing.

As his eyes grew accustomed to the night he made out a figure in the middle of the road, moaning in pain. It was a man. He had been on a bicycle, which now lay crumpled beside him. He was struggling to drag himself and the bicycle to the roadside. His legs had been smashed and there was a large pool of blood in which he slithered as he tried again and again to haul himself up. Each time he collapsed and his head fell forwards on his hands.

John Peters heard a car approaching. He rushed to where the man lay and, standing before him, raised both arms as if to be crucified.

The headlights snapped round the corner, blinding him. He was almost deafened by the screech of brakes and skidding as the car swerved. It missed them narrowly and vanished into the night.

John Peters began pulling the man towards the kerb. He was very heavy, and insisted on clutching the mangled bicycle. It was difficult to achieve a foothold on the slithery tar macadam.

But the injured man was almost there when another car rounded the corner at high speed. In the sudden brilliance of oncoming headlights John Peters again threw up both arms and was blinded.

There was a crash. An explosion. After overwhelming noise, silence. After violent movement, absolute stillness.

18

They wheeled John Peters on a hospital trolley into a long, harshly lit corridor. They left him next to a small room where two nurses were at work. One was saying, 'I think she mad. She done drunk some hot drinks with the sleeping-pill.'

Meanwhile they shaved between the legs of a man who had been made to lie back in a curious contraption, his feet wide apart and dangling from crutches to give his anal area maximum exposure. The nurses chatted and giggled, telling each other stories. When the man's testicles dropped, one of the nurses firmly popped them up again, without interrupting her conversation. The other said casually to the man, 'Here is to cover yourself', and gave him the end of the sheet. The man only grunted.

'What for you go there?' the first nurse asked.

Her friend replied, 'So I can know that place.'

'That place is too cold.'

When they had finished shaving the man, a medical orderly entered and said, 'I'll check him up', and left with the patient.

There were noises off that sounded like labour pains.

Afterwards the nurses pushed John Peters on his ambulatory bed into the small room. There was a dank smell and a smell of rubber. Beside the empty contraption lay an assortment of appliances.

The girls went back into the corridor. One said, 'Can I off de light?'

*

General Martin saw Brendan Murphy standing on the sea-
ward side of the hotel after breakfast. He told him the news.

'What on earth happened?' asked Brendan in alarm.

'Hit-and-run accident, as I understand it. Might even have
been the army. These things happen all the time, especially
with the black-out.'

'But what could he have been doing down on the Esplanade?'

'Don't rightly know.'

'At that hour of night.'

'I think he had a girl-friend there.'

'But in the street?'

'No idea.'

'Will he be all right?'

'Can't be sure yet. He hasn't recovered consciousness.'

'Is he very badly injured?'

'From what the hospital says, it's pretty bad.'

'Poor bastard.'

In the silence that followed Brendan thought he saw in the
distance an African fishing-boat putting out, but in the glare
of the sun reflected off the water he could not be sure and his
eyes were a little moist.

General Martin noticed neither. He said, 'Hear you're off.
When do you leave?'

'As soon as I've handed over to the next man.'